Prologue

Zerachiel was the last Being Zeus expected to see at day's end. In fact, he was rather unhappy he came to him, especially unannounced. But as the Angel's emotions were apathetic to the qualities of consideration, there was no need in arguing.

After greeting each other, the two set foot to the dining area, gold amassing the majority of the decorations down the corridor. There wasn't a single place left without Zeus' face, or his vigorous structure on it. But one statue stood out in particular to Zerachiel; Zeus' beloved stance holding his scepter.

Hera and Io came floating in after the men. It was a shame that Hera still pretended to love her husband. Even when Zeus neglected her love, and laid down with Io every night. It didn't matter if they hadn't had children, Hera lost her place to a human.

Io stared blankly at Zeus' third wife. She couldn't waste her time fighting over him. Especially when there was always someone greater to love.

Zerachiel played with his goblet, first covering his mouth with it. Then he turned it bottom side up on the table, and spun it. In amusement, the Angel watched it tumble off on to the floor.

Typical of his presence after dinner, Hera and Io excused themselves. But Io turned to give an ear as Zeus closed the door completely. It was his hope no one else would hear.

"What's the worst that could happen?" Zerachiel asked.

"Once they're released, they'll destroy Olympus in search of me, then make their way to Earth. It's too much to risk," Zeus said, combing through his silver lined beard.

"I suppose everything I've worked so hard to achieve will be lost. The annihilation of your betray filled humans…and worse….snobbish angels…snuffed out. Just like that?" Zerachiel cooed, "I expected more from you."

"If you do summon them, the blood will be on your hands," Zeus implied.

"I'll bathe in it every day to prove my point," Zerachiel hissed.

Zeus sighed, and looked to the door. He swore he had secured it, and there it was, propped open just enough for someone to hear. Panicking, he stood, but saw Zerachiel gesturing for his scepter.

Glazed in gold, and on display…this wasn't something Zeus allowed anyone to simply play with. But he was indebted to Zerachiel. So the answer was yes.

The grinning Angel carefully pulled it off of its stand, and swung it, the longest point directed towards Zeus. Gulping, the god sat back down, still eyeballing the door.

"I need the View of the Deities, sir. I know what to do after that…" the Angel demanded, smiling at the Trident.

Exasperating, Zeus walked to the door, hoping the person had left. But there sat Io, crouching in her sleep wear. She smiled innocently as her husband examined her, then she snapped her attention to Zerachiel.

He glowed down at her as well, which was odd to Zeus. Acting coy, Io put her head down, and walked off. Before she turned the corner down the hall, she maneuvered to get a last glimpse of Zeus. Or was it Zerachiel she had eyes for?

As Zerachiel stepped onto the map, Zeus started to doubt his intelligence with this treaty. Zerachiel promised to spare Zeus' life, even though heaven was after it. In fact, this Angel told him that he had pulled a few strings. There was nothing for him to concern himself with.

Zeus mulled this over, trying not to show how fearful he was. Heaven was ruled by God, and since Zerachiel was His creation…shouldn't his death be God's decision? Not to mention the Archangel of Death would be dispatched…who has taken the fall in the place of his life?

Heavily in thought, Zeus failed to notice what Zerachiel had already done. The small box centered in the map was open, and a black smoke began swirling to the sky. With a breeze flowing by, it swept the smoke up, dispersing it further.

The deed had been done. Zeus' hope now was that no one noticed the ground tremble, or hear the loud explosion heard from the sea. He was sure of one thing, Zerachiel needed to be stopped.

Later that night, Zeus felt his bed shift, then his eyes followed his quiet lover as she slipped out of the room. He rose to keep watch on her, only to peek his head around the corner.

At first, it was hard to gather what they were doing. The curtains that topped every pillar fluttered in the night breeze. They danced and shifted two shapes forming in the darkness. But there, in the shadows of the hall, Zerachiel embraced Io, then locked lips with her.

She melted into Zerachiel, then began lifting up her gown to the touch of his hand. They panted, and groped each other, until Zerachiel had her pinned against a pillar.

"What else is there?" he asked, still standing down the hall.

Io pushed Zerachiel off, then ran to Zeus. But he backed up, hesitant to her arrival. Io smiled at his anger. It seemed as though she enjoyed watching his temper flare.

"It's nothing…" she said, trying to calm her husband, "just touching and kissing…things we don't do…"

"I realize haven't been the best husband, Io, but we are still married…" Zeus said.

Io laughed, putting her hand to her mouth at her ignorance. This angered him even more so, and hot tears began to develop from his weak eyes.

"Zeus," she giggled, "you've cheated on me and all your other wives so many times, I figured you wouldn't mind."

Nothing to say to that. He couldn't defend himself on that regard. But he stood there with Io, glaring down the hall at Zerachiel, who shrugged and stretched his shoulders, then glared back at Zeus.

And Zeus could have sworn a shot of red displayed across his eyes. His temple vibrated once Zerachiel made his leave, then he gave his attention to his scandalous wife.

"Zeus," she started, "We've never had sex. It was mostly kissing. I haven't given myself to you, I'd never give myself to any man…"

"It doesn't matter," Zeus said, "I won't be here for you to care."

Zeus hoped this Angel of Death would come for his life. It would be better than living with the knowledge of Zerachiel's plan. But usually, the Angel of Death completed his jobs. Zeus has lost several children under his hand. And, without a trace.

This troubled, mighty god was now sitting a the edge of his realm, over looking Earth. He used to stand here to welcome the day for his followers. That had been centuries ago. The sun began to crest over the Eastern edge, as clouds swirled from his view of the below. If only he had wings like this Angel….

This Azrael was standing on the highest cliff in the world, staring out in despair. His fists were clinched, his jaw muscles rigid as he closed in on the chaos trembling through the world. He would flinch at the sound of a woman screaming while a man stabbed at her, the blaring of sirens else where, rescuing a child who may not make it. Gun shots clicked in a pattern as the victims of their aim cried out in anguish.

And then in a crisp wisp of motions, this magnificent Being snapped his wings, and boomed upward, shredding the clouds in his ascent.

Azrael was the Archangel of Death. And heaven proclaimed, he had been the best.

Would you sleep if you had killed someone?

Chapter One: I dream of Angels

I sat up quickly, panicking. The air in my lungs had been stifled as I coughed and choked to inhale. Crazy how a dream always seems so realistic, right? So much, that my heart labored with short breaths as the anxiety began jolting throughout my body. I was rather hot and drenched in sweat, a sign I'd been fighting to live. Is there a mental condition for someone attracted to their assailant?

What a shame that his obvious intent was murder. Tragic to me, since this Being had been absolutely *gorgeous*. A great talent of mine had to be forgetting bad dreams…Or so I thought. But, not only had it been pretty terrifying, it was rare for me to have one at all.

Everything seemed to be running along fine until I opened the door to the room where the chess matches were being held. I felt someone was watching me. Being that I am a goddess though, why was this strange?

I walked back and forth, assuring the chess tables were set and perfect as I tried to shrug off this growing manifestation of insanity. *I couldn't see them, even if this were possibly true.*

I shivered at that regard, but I couldn't let this ruin my day. Resetting the timers came up next on my tasks. After that I sat down with my laptop and made sure each one was connected. It was irritating to me that these clocks were wirelessly operated during the match.

Peter came in through the door, smelling fresh and smiling. He nodded at me and started setting down registration cards for our young players to fill out. Once he finished, he stood back to see if everything was perfect, then began to meddle with the tables again.

In my opinion, he was either gay or suffered horribly from O.C.D. I studied his demeanor for a moment and shook my head. Peter looked in my direction with his eyebrows raised. But I smiled at him, and excused myself.

Making my way into the bathroom seemed to be a struggle. Before I made it to the door I had five men gawk, stutter, introduce themselves then ask me out. I was over blushing since they had no idea of my age. As I washed my hands I thought to myself that staring in the mirror didn't do much for me...(since I've been staring at the same face for thousands of years.)

Being immortal had its perks. But believe or not, *it got old*. I was, however, in love with myself. With eyes that were bright green, and dark brown wavy hair...standing at 5'10'' gave me that unwanted attention a lot of mortal women crave.

Instinctively speaking, I hated attention. I have had too many things to do in my life to concern myself with the compliments I've heard in different languages. Living for thousands of years will show you how fickle men really are.

I pushed my lips up into a pout. As I turned to examine my jaw bone, I saw a familiar face enter. Smiling at Ashleigh, I noticed she had her makeup bag partially opened. She spilled the messy contents on the sink, and grinned at me.

"Whitney!" she exclaimed, searching through dirty tissues and pencil shavings, "You look so pretty!"

"Thanks...Ashleigh."

She was a sweet girl, but she's called a ketchup stain "pretty" before. Answering dryly *sometimes* made her stop speaking, however she was used to my responses.

I watched her apply eye shadow, and then in a clumsy manner she began to clump on massive amounts of mascara. Laughing a little, I handed her the lip gloss that was about to roll onto the floor when I noticed the name.

"The only secret I can think this Victoria might have would be she's either a man, or her boobs are fake," I said, trying to make her laugh.

She snorted and nodded in the mirror as she twisted gel up into her bird's nest. Then she molded the rest of it into a pony tail.

"Or both," she said, trying to add to my joke.

The superior concept in my mindset was automatic; I smiled but deep down inside I wish she hadn't added that part. Once she had finished we both made our way back to the room. I jumped in shock when I realized the twins had made their way in.

It wasn't so much Rachel and Randall were there...It was more so their existence...period. And to my knowledge, only three people were allowed to judge this match. I smiled at them then looked at Peter and Ashleigh in agitation. They both shrugged and continued to greet our arriving contestants.

As the seats behind the white line started to fill, I grabbed a clipboard with the players names and began to pair them up with their opponent. For hours these kids would square off until the last one was left.

To the other volunteers, these kids were sheer terror. Although they were held high in intelligence, they were still seventeen and under. It also didn't help that their hormones were on a tight rope.

I felt it was unfair to match the girls up with the boys. In my mind, it was a natural female tendency to be patient. But...the last two players were out of my control. I winked at Melissa as she peered through her thick spectacles. Then I showed the players to their tables.

After twenty minutes, one player was eliminated; he had used his best plays first. I watched him sacrifice the most important pieces. As a volunteer, we weren't allowed to give them advice, although I was sure I held more experience in this area-without any effort.

Stopping over a match, I watched the younger girl completely beguile her opponent. The instant she snapped out of her trance, she hit the clock and grinned at her seventeen year old rival. Heather looked up in shock, then off to the audience while trying to remain calm. She stood slowly, choking back her over-spilled drama and nodded as she walked away.

I winked at Leslie as well and strolled off. Strategy was key in a successful win while playing chess. You were watching a silent war of marble unfold underneath your fingertips; the outcome depends on every single move you make.

After a couple of hours, only four players remained. Little Melissa was sweeping over the competition effortlessly. Then there was Jeremy, the oldest boy. He skimmed his hand over the board, taking a mental note of all of his pieces. Once he made his final move, he smiled and hit the timer.

Then at last it was Melissa and Jeremy. A droplet of swear smudged it's way down his forehead. His long, pale fingers dangled over the board as he made his final move. Apathetic, and in for the kill, Melissa finished the match with a fierce look in her eye. Then she hit the timer, and stood to curtsey.

Having a hard time hiding his emotion, Jeremy stood anyway to shake Melissa's hand. And as the applause steadied, he rushed off, heading towards his parents.

Randall came behind me with his clipboard. As the crowds started to part, I found it in my best interests to glare at him. Our staring match was interrupted when I fixed my glance to my approaching father. *Of all places at all times*. Randal studied my face, then took a deep breath.

"The woes of being a family," he said, trying to add humor to my disgust.

How strange was it that Randal figured we were related? In the hopes to exclude him in our conversation I turned and smiled gingerly.

"Fortunately, you and I are not…" I said.

His brows knitted together in defeat, and pleased with his reaction I turned to attend to my father.

There he was, looming over the chess boards, pointing at certain pieces, and watching them shatter as a spark of lightening flew from his finger. *Of course*, he was completely ignoring the fact that people might notice. A few jumped in shock, attempting to move away, though still enamored by the stupidity my father put on display. I ran over to him and pressed his arm to his side then looked him in his face.

"How old are you again?" I asked under my breath, "we have to replace anything we break…and some of these pieces are actual marble!"

A small group passing by stared in bewilderment at my father. He smiled childishly, and as soon as he opened his mouth, I intervened.

"He dropped his cigarette…on his lighter," I lied, squinting my eyes.

A few nodded at me, but I could tell they were skeptical of us. Who cared if he was Zeus, it made no matter to me; it was how he always acted. And as predicted, Rachel asked if everything was okay. Then she began to push the remaining guests out of the door.

I gestured to shoo her away. Then I became even more irritated when I saw Peter's eyes all over my father in curiosity. I motioned for him and Ashleigh to close the last few doors, then turned to my man child.

"What do you want!" I asked him impatiently.

"I miss my daughter, isn't that a natural fatherly tendency?"

"Not for someone who has a countless number of wives, mistresses, and bastard children!"

The squeaking of someone's shoes made both of us pause and look up. Melissa was standing at the door waiting for her parents. This I would handle later. I pulled down on my father's arm again and moved closer to his ear.

"I'll come home around spring to visit. But I'm not staying long. And I don't want to stay in your temple!" I whispered while pulling him to the exit.

He stalled to gave me a sad look. A feeling of deprecation erupted suddenly; we both knew he didn't care. He was a god, and if anything else the most selfish of them all. In my mind I figured if he felt deprived, why not find a nymph or a mistress of his? Why take the time to bother me?

After pushing him out of the door, I turned to Melissa and grabbed her hand. Her parents had a bad habit of waiting in the front. Once we met them near the entrance, her mother attempted to hand me twenty dollars. I nodded politely but turned the money down. That's when I looked into Melissa's eyes.

"Tell them," I whispered, nudging her slightly.

"I won today," Melissa started off.

Both of her parents were quiet and uneasy, but her father patted me on the shoulder.

"Good bye," she said to me, waving.

A sad feeling began to flourish as I watched this rather faux family walk off. They were always so rigid, and I found it rude they never spoke. Of course, Melissa has told me so much that every time I see them, my hidden intent is to quarrel. I'm not impulsive, but it is quite tempting.

Sorry for seeming vague, *I am* Enyo, the goddess of war. Most people tend to generalize what my purpose is. My main objective would be to help an opponent choose the correct strategy. This helps reduce the cost of weapons, time, and most importantly, life. I give generals the wisdom many have referred to as geniuses.

My job doesn't make me "the goddess" of death, who is actually my older sister. Death can come at any time. Keres' job is to insure you do die in battle. Whether by sword, by a gun, or by someone you love.

Supposedly, all of the god's and goddess' powers counteract the other. Athena is the goddess of wisdom; she is the first born, and my oldest sister. As much as we love each other, she tells me on a daily basis that she loathes my job. Well, she tells me whenever I go home to visit…

Soon I was enraged with doubt, and decided to contact my father. I was now sitting at my desk with both of my hands down pressing against the hardwood. The globe I used to communicate through realms had a thick layer of dust on it. It was obvious I wasn't one for family reunions.

In order to contact Hermes I always felt I had to trick him. Either with a lie or saying that I missed him (sometimes by making it sound like something was urgent.) He always read my letters that traveled back home, so there really was no need in doing this.

"Hermes, I have a letter for you," I said, speaking into my globe.

As quick as a breath he entered my study. The light that arrived before him set off the fire alarm…as usual. I stood up on my chair and fanned it until the beeping stopped. Then I jumped off and looked at him while trying to seem melancholy.

"I have a letter that needs to be sent," I said, looking for a pen and paper.

"No need to write it down. Just tell me what it is, and I'll be sure to pass it along," Hermes said, walking towards me.

I looked up and brushed the hair in my eyes away. Then I smiled. I figured no matter how much syrup I poured on it, he would discover what I had written. So playing him up might be my only option. I tried to pout as I sighed deeply, and put my hands in the pockets of my dress making sure he saw my face was downcast.

"Just go," he said, pushing my shoulder, "There's no need to say you won't. He'll just keep bothering you until you do."

"Damn," I said under my breath, adjusting my dress, "and how do you know he came to visit me?"

"He recently paid visits to a few others, and letters have been flying back and forth. I don't read theirs; however, I read yours…"

"Why?" I asked, rushing out of my room to fetch a glass of wine. *A huge glass of wine.*

"I cannot discuss that matter with you," he said, a step behind me, "it would most certainly risk the relationship between you and our father."

Because that wasn't falling apart what so ever…

"So you watch me, but you're a messenger?" I asked, pouring out the remaining contents into my glass, "Do you want some?"

"I don't drink," he said to me with a straight face, "And you are my younger sister. Yes, Enyo. I watch you…"

I laughed at his answer and took a big gulp before setting the glass on the counter. Then I leaned against it and crossed my arms. Hermes seemed tense, and to say the least, more unstable than he usually was. I examined him prior to turning my head towards the front door.

"I'm the goddess of war….not sensual pleasures. If it were Aphrodite's glass…"

"Isn't sexual intercourse sometimes considered a war? And I can't leave until you give me a message to send to our father," he said calmly.

"Well, tell him he can expect me around spring. Like I've already told him."

"Time is not your friend at the moment, Enyo. It's better you come as soon as possible," Hermes said.

He indeed was not acting natural. Hermes' eyes were all over my apartment as if he were nervous. He had his hands neatly planted on my counter, but he kept shifting his stance. Then his eyes met with mine again as I offered him my final answer.

"Fine," I said, hoping he would leave, "I'll be there in a week."

"It's better. But…"

"Since when do you care?" I asked, allowing my temper to flare, "Relay my message to our father and leave it at that!"

Hermes nodded, and then walked to my door. He reached for the knob, but instead of walking out he vanished into the bright light that he came in. I grabbed a magazine to fan the fire alarm above the door when I noticed a small piece of parchment on my floor.

As the smoke and flames died around the edges, I picked it up and read. Utterly confused, I sat the paper on the counter and downed my glass. Then I made my way over to the couch. I didn't feel like watching TV, so I laid back, resting my head on the mountain of pillows I had displayed.

Five minutes dwelled by, when I shot up and looked around. Teiresias was seated at the adjacent chair near my back door. Since he was blind I did not call out his name but I sat in silence, shocked at his arrival.

"Enyo," he said calmly, "I fear us meeting will not go well."

"Isn't that a stereotypical line for everyone?" I said, mocking him.

"Miscommunication and deceit lies in the house from which you were born."

This was nothing new; however, Teiresias never said anything about my family.

"For who is amassed in deceitfulness will never admit it, but has cast you from his protection. There is much he has hidden," he continued, "and your life in this realm will come to an end."

Ignoring this banter from Teiresias, I asked that he departed. Then I laid my head down to sleep. As soon as I closed my eyes, there he was, the most amazing Being I had ever seen. I smiled, feeling comforted as he walked my way.

My eyes danced with his once he drew closer. As he turned to face me, his expression changed, and I felt my heart beat out of control. Soon this beauty was at my throat, reciting a piece for someone who was assigned to kill.

Unable to move and stumped at my attraction to him, I watched his wings develop from his back. Regardless of my fear, I watched a single feather tracing its travel, slowly floating to the ground. Then I looked back to him, hoping he saw the pain across my face.

This Angel's eyes gleamed with anger as he lifted his right arm. I remained silent, choked up in disbelief. My fear had vanished, and I now resented anything I had ever done. Tears began to spill from my eyes, and onto his arm. Without question he was staring into them, watching me die. It wasn't a look of satisfaction, either, but of pure regret. He seemed astonished with his actions.

I sat up from the couch and nearly fell. Pressing my hand against my chest, I tried to breathe. That was the most horrifying vision of him since the dreams began. He was out to kill me. But since it was a reverie, I calmed myself down.

In doing this, I stood up and located my phone on the kitchen counter. I couldn't think of anything else to do but go back to sleep. As soon as I laid down, I drifted off once again. Even if I had the same dream, *it was only an illusion*.

One thing I couldn't seem to brush off…Teiresias' words vibrating in my head.

Chapter Two: Heaven's Assassin

As the only Archangel of Death, I am dispatched to hunt murderers; it is always a fallen deity with the taste for blood. My objective is redundant. *Kill those who kill*. It is not the will of God, but since the fall of man, it's the only way to keep balance.

Sitting and watching your victim was just about as fun as watching thirty seconds worth of horrible sex. To be realistic, I was almost sure I'd rather watch him displease yet another woman, than watch him down seven shots of crap.

I've been following this demigod for four months and still haven't find an open opportunity to relay my message to him. After exploring several options of taking him out, I settled on a sniper's point of view-at least for now.

I figured since most of the people around him were unaware of who he was, it was best I did this alone and without anyone else's knowledge. He parted ways with his guests. Then he clumsily walked upstairs with a dark haired ditz that had been riding his nuts all night. (I knew this wouldn't last long.)

After three minutes of nothing, I aimed my rifle in his direction to take a shot, but noticed the girl decided to stay. Pissed at her decision, I slammed my gun down and stood up. The night breeze was cold as it swirled the inexorable scent of car emissions around. *What a disgusting place to live.*

Descending off of this building would be a quicker option, but being how big this city was…someone would see me. Instead I took the elevator, and crossed over to his tower. The lady that worked the front desk was helping me keep tabs on him, though I'm not sure why.

When I walked into the lobby, she smiled as if she were happy to see me. But tonight I ignored her. Lately her v cut shirts were getting lower. Or, she was talking about her ex boyfriend. Since I'm not him, and I didn't care in the first place…she was wasting her breath. Setting another plan in motion, I pulled out my phone to text my pal, Nathan.

Waiting outside wasn't to my benefit. It had gotten colder, and my friend was late. After about twenty minutes, I turned and watched my target, Mitchell, drag his drunken friend out of the elevator. Then they posted up on the furniture while he called a cab. He caught a glimpse of me, but Mitchell pretended he didn't see I was standing outside.

I nodded at Nathan as he pulled up with the cab. He got out and slapped me on the shoulder. Then he lit a cigarette as soon as he stepped onto the sidewalk. Nathan only did this when he was nervous.

"Four months, A.Z.?" he said, releasing a large cloud of smoke in my face.

I shuddered at the smell, and adjusted my jacket's collar.

"He's either having sex or with his mom," I answered dryly, stepping into the cab.

I hit the horn and waited for Mitchell to bring his friend out. As Nathan and I both predicted, the young woman pursued him to come home with her. My target agreed as he got in. I nodded once she gave me the street address, then I began to drive off.

With my luck, the girl he agreed to go home with talked entirely too much. That and the perfume she wore murdered my sinuses. I opened the window to get some air, and realized how close we were to their destination. Once we pulled up, I saw Nathan standing outside talking to a woman. He gestured at me, and in an instant he disappeared.

The girl spilled out of the cab first, and then my target attempted to pay me. Without a second thought, I hit the gas on the vehicle and began to speed down the street. Nathan rolled into the back out of nowhere, and shut the door behind him.

"What the hell!" Mitchell exclaimed as he backed into the right side of the cab.

"Exactly," I said, turning into an alley.

I pulled the car into an abandoned factory and as I exited, knocked on the roof of it. Nathan shot into the air with Mitchell in his hands. Then he dropped him about six feet onto the vehicle, and descended slowly next to me.

Ignoring his groans of pain, I popped the trunk open and began to sort through my folders until I came across his file. Then I spread out the hundreds of photos of all his murder victims. The last girl he killed was only 18 years old. She had just graduated high school and invited him to her graduation. After a few drinks, they made their way back to his house.

Typical story. Wrong place, wrong guy kind of thing. I situated all of the photos on the trunk, then motioned Nathan to retrieve him. Nathan pulled Mitchell's head back and slammed his face down on the back of the cab.

"I need a reason before I kill you," I said sternly.

"For what?" he asked, trying to wiggle free.

"For the murders you've committed," I said, searching for a container.

He attempted to push up from the trunk, but Nathan slammed his face down again. Then Mitchell began to plead. How sad was it that he's killed as many people as he has, but when death comes knocking, his requisition is mercy?

Sorry, I'm apathetic by nature.

Once I located my capsule, I noted that one pill was left. Since I was at close range, shooting him would create a mess. I carefully removed it from the canister and smiled at him. He remained confused, but I wasn't done explaining myself.

"I can't tell you who I am, but I will remind you of this. Killing is a sin. However, you can be forgiven. But..." I said, motioning to Nathan, "killing and assuming you're better than God, your creator...that's a huge misstep."

"So you're judging me?" he asked, still trying to slip from Nathan's grip, "isn't that His job?"

"Oh...I'm not judging you. I don't have that right. But if He feels your time is up, that's where I step in," I answered.

"No one can judge anyone except God," Nathan said, struggling to keep his grip.

He looked at me in frustration, then thumbed Mitchell's jaw open.

"Don't chew or crush this pill. Let it dissolve," I said, slipping it on the side of his cheek.

Nathan pressed his hand over Mitchell's mouth as his eyes began to roll in the back of his head. Once we were sure it dissipated, I sat most of my paper work back into the folder then handed it to Nathan. He stuffed it into his coat and nodded at me. Then he walked towards the exit and in a flash he disappeared.

I watched Mitchell writhe in pain for a moment, when I realized how much I abhorred my purpose. Finding murderers and killing them had lost its thrill.

His complexion quickly transcended to a dark purple, and as I checked his pulse before closing his jaundiced eyes, I prayed for my actions. I skimmed through his information I left for myself, and sited him as perished. Then I slid into the driver's seat, and drove off.

One to two days from now, heaven would send a messenger angel to give me another assignment. Another reason to loathe my objective had to be how the world got worse every day. People now openly kill their children. Men murder other men over money-or for no reason at all. People take their lives at their own hand in the attempts to escape the insanity of this life. I felt in some way I added to the unbalance of this place.

Being a deity *never* had its perks, especially not for my line of work. But I know for a fact I couldn't be God. He is patient with his creations, and He has been patient with His angels. He loves every single one of the humans on Earth, no matter what they do. That is true compassion that I'm sure most people don't realize. To me, an Angel…it seemed out of reach.

I slowly pulled up in front of my house then walked to the door but stopped when I heard the flutter of wings. I looked over at the tree near my neighbor's and noticed an owl perched on an upper most branch. *It wasn't strange that this animal had been there for three weeks in a row*….Same branch, same tree. And no matter what time I came home, he was there.

He sat silently, but would stretch out his wings and move his head from side to side. At first I wondered if he had been injured, but he always flew off once I entered my house.

Sometimes I hoped it was Zerachiel, but he always came as himself. Though he disciplined his emotional reactions, I wish his facial expression did change. Maybe he needed a voice synthesizer….you could hear the disgust when Zerachiel spoke. In fact, he's been *displeased* with me since I've been established down to Earth.

The seniority of the Angels can be compared to how a company runs; whoever has been there longer, and has done greater things. It depends on your job and your purpose. Angels that sing or write are held in higher esteem than me.

Even Angels who are just plain Angels are considered better than I am. Messenger Angels are close to being the best. They provide messages to humans and other Angels. But all heavenly hosts follow the same rules.

We are not allowed to interact with a mortal or other immortals. This includes no sexual intercourse, no emotional transferring (unless otherwise instructed), and we can love them, but we cannot covet them. Since we aren't the Creator, our flesh is weak. *Just like a mortal*.

I stared at the clock above my stove waiting for dawn. At that time, I could fly over to the ridge of the mountains. There I could sit at the highest point to watch the sun rise. It was the only thing that seemed to make sense to me.

I could never question my God, or Zerachiel, though I've sometimes wanted to. There are other Angels that have been cast out of heaven, and now live here on Earth, or in hell. It isn't because heaven is hiding something; it's what an Angel would do with what they find.

Nathan called my cell phone a few minutes before I decided to leave, sounding disappointed. He was typically tense before and after an assignment, but last night went a little rough for him.

"I didn't want to kill him in front of that girl," I said, trying to calm him down, "we can't have witnesses."

"She wouldn't swallow the pill I gave her," he hissed, "I almost had to hurt her."

"Did she remember anything?" I asked, spinning an orange on my counter.

"No."

"Then stop worrying."

Exasperating, he hung up. I suppose the only plus side to being heaven's assassin had to be the disintegration of the body. The pill dispensed to Mitchell stops all bodily functions. And soon after his flesh and bones evaporate into the air, leaving nothing behind.

Recalling my first assignment always followed with nightmares. Even though it didn't take long for the poison to work, watching someone's body fall to pieces isn't the best thing to experience.

The first bird began to chirp when realized I was late. I ran into my back yard then flew into the air. In no time I neared the mountain's summit and I arrived just as the sun began to rise. It gave a promise to always be bright and warm. The sun's accession was slow at first, it then sped up as the moon seemed to be nothing but a fading sliver.

Everything became illuminated, and the shadows began to melt into light. I wish I could forget everything, like a sun rise shining my memory clean. I stared off into the distance a moment longer as I ascended up to fly back home. I landed in my front yard and walked up to the door.

The hardest part of being immortal would be having to move. I've relocated over a thousand times in the last two hundred years. Since there was a new generation evolving often, I've found myself in places I used to live. To mount on top of never making more than one friend, I've killed nearly two million Beings in my lifetime. But I've never killed a woman.

I'm not sure I would be able to do it. It would also depend on what she had done. The majority of the people I'm sent to kill are super humans. About three fourths of the people I've killed have murdered twenty to thirty times more than I have.

One man claimed he had no idea of what he was doing. But because he kept moving around the world, it was hard to believe. It's not hard killing someone that deserves to die. It's difficult forgetting about what they've done their whole entire life.

The other fourth of my victims are typical humans. Serial killers, mass rapist/murderers. They don't move. They don't run. And they never see death coming. The problem with demigods, super humans, or if you wish, gods and goddesses-they have soothsayers and oracles that warn them when their life was in peril.

This makes it harder to track them. Mortals don't even realize when a demigod or deity is in the room. But I can. They generate a different type of energy than humans do. Most of the time it's dark, especially if they kill to get by.

Sleeping wasn't an option. I only slept when I was upset. So I showered then combed my hair back. I found my apron then located my name badge. Just because you're immortal doesn't mean you shouldn't work. And oh, how I loved cutting meat all day.

I figured since I've had about three thousand years of hacking at chunks of meat, it was better to settle with being a butcher. On the other hand, I never got any satisfaction from cutting cow rump. It was already dead by the time it made it to the meat locker. No need to explain the job. Just enjoy the cut of meat you buy from my selection.

Women flirted with me to get money taken off, and depending on the woman was depending on the price. Older women who I knew were on a fixed income received an instant discount. This also included single mothers. Single women who were flirtatious and clearly set on having a sexual relationship were turned to my coworker, April.

She was sinister, apathetic, nonsocial on purpose, and extremely attractive. There were too many times I caught myself thinking about her, and had to ask for forgiveness. Hard to not watch her. She was average height, with dark brown hair, and almond shaped eyes. She had a collection of freckles neatly scattered across her nose and upper cheeks. Sometimes, when business was slow, I would watch her walk around. Slow motion, even if she were switching price labels.

However, there was one thing that kept me from even mentioning how beautiful she was; April was lesbian. I never asked her how she decided it was okay, but meeting the father of her two kids gave me enough for a theory.

I walked into the back-room and watched her watching me. She smiled sweetly as I opened my locker to store my personal items. Then she stood to face me as she always did, and rested her hands on my shoulders.

"A guy as gorgeous as you should smile once in a while," she said, rubbing them.

"I'll smile when I don't have to do what I do," I said.

"What do you do? Strip for a living?" she said, rubbing my arms.

"Something that is associated with the night life…thing," I answered.

"We can tell you don't go out," she laughed, helping me with my tie.

April combed her fingers through my black hair as she did every morning. I moved her hands and looked at the small broken mirror next to the lockers.

"I want it combed back," I said, undoing her style.

"Why! You look mysterious, A.Z.…." she said.

"Well, I want to look professional. Please don't give these women any more reasons to hit on me…"

She nodded at my remark and watched me fix my hair. A small piece decided it didn't want to remain with the rest of my do, but I didn't have time to reconstruct it. We both shuffled into the manager's office, clocked in, then pushed each other out to the meat locker. I grabbed the first coat I saw then opened the back door to wait for the delivery man.

He was either late, or early but playing with his iPad. Today he was late, and today it was supposed to snow. I sighed and watched my breath crystallize as it hit the air. April rested her chin on my shoulder and stared out of the door with me. Outside of Nathan, she was the closest I had to a family here on Earth.

"So…did you go out with that girl," she asked, dusting something dark purple off of my shoulder.

"Yes. And then I took her back to my house to watch movies," I said, recalling that evening.

"And then?"

"I took her home!" I exclaimed, turning around.

"You didn't…"

"I can't," I said, noticing her reaction.

"What's so bad with sex?" she asked out of curiosity, "You never talk about the hot tail you nailed with the other guys. Are you a virgin?"

"Yes, and I have to stay that way for the rest of my life."

"Are you a monk?" she said, grinning.

"I told you, I'm under oath. I took a vow and cannot break it, no matter what."

"Even if you were in love?" she said, her brows slightly knitted.

"If I ever could love, yes. Even then," I answered, pushing her shoulder, "why do you care so much?"

"I'm practically the sister you never asked for. I can harass you if I want," she responded, "And besides, I'm worried about you. You've been quiet lately."

Answering her did nothing for either of us. She had no idea I was Azreal, the Archangel of Death. She didn't need to know either. I felt it would ruin our friendship. And besides, I had to move within the next couple of years, or I would be 26 years old for 7 years in a row. I smirked at her, and then turned to the door when I heard the delivery guy. April jumped and walked off once she heard our manager screaming my name.

Since the delivery guy was only ten minutes late, I decided not to reprimand him. I signed for the meat, checked it, and then helped him haul it onto the hangers. Once we were done, I took my coat off and walked over to the sink to wash my hands. I noticed dark purple ash around the faucet and wondered if someone had been smoking near it. Ignoring my discovery I walked to the front of deli department to the shrill sound of our manager's voice.

My boss was short and chubby with beady eyes. Her hair was thinning, and her skin stayed greasy. Patricia had the most irritating voice I've ever come across in my life. And…you've guessed it…she could never seem to be silent. She continued barking at April as she watched me walk around to turn the light on for the display. Then her eyes followed me when I walked behind the counter to reset the scale.

"Was he late?" she said, huffing in my direction.

I nodded, trying not to interact with her. Lately she talks to me, just to stare at me. Or tell me "how darn cute you are." Ignoring her, I began to notice our first customer every Tuesday, Martin. Martin never spoke. He pointed at what he wanted, and then nodded. So…Martin was my best friend. I didn't like talking to the customers anyway.

The only thing about Martin…he wore the same hat, same coat, same shirt….you get the picture. And he always bore such a tart scent. I twisted up my nose as he scanned the display, looking at the salads and side dishes. *Since when did butchers sell salad…?* But it was Patricia's store.

He pointed, looked at me, and then pointed again. As usual I was right. I gestured to April as I handed him his food. He nodded and walked over to her register. Then I slumped against the counter and pulled out my phone. I have no one to text or call; I just like playing angry birds. Sometimes I ignored the customers that came up, who will usually yell at me before they would walk down to April. As I said before, I don't talk much.

A piece of paper flew at me from the other side of the counter. *What a typical customer gesture.* I turned around a little upset. She glared at me, and then opened her mouth to speak. But before she could I tossed the paper back.

"Thanks," I said, turning around to finish my game.

"I have a question for you," she said, tossing the paper back.

I picked it up and realized she had a pretty bad temper. So I returned her gesture just to watch her reaction. She pressed her lips together and glared at me again as she tossed it back. It bounced off of my forehead and flew into an open display window, fitting in perfectly with the shabbily made potato salad. *I'm almost sure no one would notice.*

"What?" I asked, returning her menacing look.

"It's yes…" she said, glaring even harder.

"*Yes?*"

"Where's the bathroom?" she said.

If my eyebrows knitted any closer, you might mistake I owned a uni-brow. She really harassed me all this time over the restroom. I guided her through the store, looking back to see if she were still behind me. At one point I found myself examining her.

She was tall and her body was *definitely* well defined. She had long, dark brown wavy hair, and huge, bright green eyes. Everything on her face was perfectly structured-well...everything on her was perfectly structured. She nodded as I pointed the rest of the way. But I was curious to know who she was. I watched her walk, when I realized I was hypnotized by the movement of her hips...

Outside of April, there weren't too many woman as attractive as this. Something was odd about that.

I heard faint mumbling once she was inside the bathroom. Then a bright light conveyed from the cracks surrounding the door. My immediate reaction was to open it, but once I did she had already vanished. All that was left was a swirl of smoke, and the paper towel had caught fire.

Now I'm positive she wasn't human.

Without mentioning it, I took my position back behind the counter while I pretended to care as an older woman prodded me about last week's cut of meat. If she had a stick with her, my hand would be bloody and bruised. Instead of reacting how I wanted, I apologized for the low quality of beef she received. It wasn't my store...it was Patricia's.

A few hours had passed and I wandered off to the ladies room to investigate. I pushed the mop bucket inside, making sure no one else was in there. Shutting the door and locking it, I began to look around. Everything seemed to be the same. No holes in the wall, ceiling, or floor.

Puzzled at my find, I halfcocked mopped the floor, then pulled the bucket back out. It was the strangest thing I noticed in years. My best guess was she was a goddess. But why teleport inside a public restroom? Wouldn't you prefer your own?

The rest of my shift went by so slow. It was my usual customers, with the usual pickup lines. Once or twice, a friend of April's tried her luck, but I couldn't keep my mind off of what I saw. Not only was she incredible, she vanished without a trace...from a filthy bathroom!

This was the most excitement I've ever had in my life! Nathan jarred me out of my thoughts when he hit the bell. He always hit the bell. I could tell it brought him joy to hit the bell. He dinged it once more, smiling at the face I was making.

"When are you off?" he asked quietly.

"In thirty minutes, why?" I asked, pulling the bell from him.

"Zerachiel wants to see you..."

"You're a Messenger Angel's messenger?" I asked, teasing him.

"He likes me more," he said, laughing as he walked away.

This was more than likely true. Zerachiel felt the way I went after my assignments was completely unorthodox. When I told him he should try it himself, he stated his purpose, how old he was, and left it at that. Ever since then he sneers when he sees me.

Soon it was time to clock out. I said good bye to April, and made my way to the alley to meet Nathan. As the cars passing by faded into the darkness, we both surged into the air, making our way to my house. I settled in my kitchen while Nathan landed on my bed. I could hear him jumping before stepping onto the floor. He sheepishly walked into the living room, and nodded at Zerachiel.

"Sorry," he said.

"Not an issue…." I said, fixing my gaze on Zerachiel.

He was sitting on one of my bar stools, his hands folded on the counter. This Messenger Angel seemed hesitant to give me the folder next to him, but pushed it towards me anyway. I read through the first few paragraphs, and slammed the folder down.

"What's new about this one? Same deal," I said, becoming annoyed.

"It's a woman."

Nathan wowed at his comment then seated himself on my couch. Zerachiel seemed less than pleased with my response and Nathan's reaction.

"It's your job, Azrael..," he said patiently, "and it has to be done. However you've been given a time frame. She's left this realm and traveled to another."

"Is she running?" I asked, opening my fridge.

"No. She's visiting her father."

"Oh, that's lovely. So she dies when she gets back?" I asked, pouring a large glass of juice.

"No."

Nathan raised his eyebrows at me and chuckled.

"I don't do well in other realms," I said, effortlessly downing my glass.

"You will have to intercept her as she returns then," Zerachiel said, standing up.

He pushed the folder into my hand, and then looked into my eyes.

"Make this one quick. You only have a month."

I flinched at his statement. Hearing that made it hard to keep a straight face.

A month wasn't long enough. Because of the confidentiality of my job, I wasn't allowed to ask why. Zerachiel ascended from my house which always made my walls rumble. Since I didn't feel like looking further into file, I tossed it to Nathan.

He opened the folder, examining the papers I threw at him. If you didn't know who Nathan was, you'd assume he was a normal guy. He mentioned to me on various occasions how plain he was. Maybe it was true, but I'm a guy. I don't check other men out. He was the same height as me, with dark hair and dark brown eyes. I figured so long as everything was in place, why worry?

He smiled a little as he sat the folder on the table and ascended into flight as well. The lights flickered once he was gone as I stared at the folder one last time. Then I retreated to my room. Because I didn't sleep, I laid awake in my bed and listened to everything around me before finding my iPod. I was in deep thought…This was my first woman as a target. Would she be easier than all the rest?

Chapter Three: As Thick as Blood

Dinner with my family was pointless. Neither of my siblings or I really had a childhood, so there wasn't much else to talk about. I noticed my mother allowed the presence of other women Zeus had impregnated. *Most of them were still alive*. I believed

Hera put up with too much and she wasn't even his first wife! She rounded the table, then sat next to me and cupped my face.

"How I've missed you, Enyo," she cooed, "why haven't you been back sooner?"

I swept a loose lock from in front of my face and smiled at my mother.

"Because…I loathe this place," I whispered back.

Apollo rounded the table as well, sitting on my left side. He looked like he wanted to say something, but I always considered him a know it all. If it's raining, he'll tell you that you may get wet, and if you get wet you'll get sick and die. Or how much it hurts to love someone who hates you, but it's better to love than hate. Sometimes I felt his birth was meaningless, but without him I'm sure my father's destruction on Earth would have been more costly.

Io joined the ranks, the distortion in her expression as fond as ash. She seemed to be more compassionate to humans. But Io seemed to forget she was simply a human that wouldn't die (almost like a pretty roach, in my opinion)… At any rate, she didn't appreciate that my sister and I called her a common whore. Sure she helped Perseus, but she helped Zeus as well…

Even after she displayed her disgust for him, she married him. I rolled my eyes at her, and traveled my attention to Metis, my father's first wife. She looked domineering, but she was always very sweet to me. In fact when my mother and Aphrodite were at each other's throats, she came around more. Metis and I smiled at each other, when my eyes darted to Aphrodite.

To me, Aphrodite's beauty was disgustingly indulging. This was my way of saying she is over rated. But of course, I'm a woman. In my eyes for someone who was considered sensual, she seemed to have a sickening effect on Apollo and me.

I don't care if she was born from sea foam, or if she was another bastard child of my father's…she was a *bitch*. She waved in our direction. As my mother, Apollo, and I waved back we sneered once she turned her head.

"Conceited tramp," Athena said under her breath.

I smiled as my sister took her place in front of me. It was good to see her. She returned my joyous gesture, and pushed a basket of rolls and grapes in my direction.

"You look gaunt," she said, trying to muster up a conversation.

"I look healthier on Earth. I'm allergic to imprudence," I retorted, "Thanks but no thanks."

Aphrodite heard what I said, and stopped her conversation to glare at me. I liked upsetting her. She was vain and everything was always about her. What I hated most about it was her support for anyone who had sex.

Unfortunately, she attracted anyone which included her siblings. She saw it as fun; we all saw it as a curse. And you can expect the worse living in a family of gods and goddess-many of the men's loins have been trapped between her thighs. She was another loveless parent with many bastard children.

The gods that were allowed in Olympus were called "Ascending Deities." Gods and goddesses such as Hades and Medusa were called Fallen Deities. They possess powers that are meant to hurt people, and blah blah blah. As I have mentioned before, being the goddess of war doesn't mean I enjoy seeing people die. In fact, I supply wisdom in fights for a more conscience battle.

Just as one plays chess, sacrificing your best moves to show bravado always ends up in fatalities. Hades is the god of death, and there are several other spirits that subdue men into recklessly killing both humans and gods…I'm not one of them.

Earth's realm and the god's realm is separated by light. We are not in the heavens, nor are we on Earth. It can almost be considered a planet. Since we were created from Super Beings, we too can die.

However, we were created out of sheer imagination, we have all been forgotten. The only others that know of us are Angels, and God himself. *Not Zeus*, God. I've never had the chance to be graced by His presence, and when I was a child my father threatened to disown me because of my curiosity.

All I had theory of would be that gods were worse than any human living. There were countless reports coming back from Earth about murderous gods and goddesses murdering innocent humans-just for the sport of it.

My question was…who was killing them?

The only way to obliterate a god came from poison on another realm that existed in this time. This realm can be considered a purgatory for gods and spirits. It is also known where a lot of the spirits Hades incorporated with were created out of the dead remains of a dying god.

I noticed I drifted from the argument my sisters started. Aphrodite was glaring Athena down, complaining about the glow of her skin. As far as I knew, Athena always glowed. Aphrodite… always seemed to dim when she was pregnant, or she had an infection…

Shaking the horrible thought from my mind, I stood up and made my way to the buffet table. Hermes was standing there, tipping an empty goblet to his mouth. He was watching my older sisters banter back and forth, but nodded when I walked up.

"Everyone in this family is inbred," he mumbled, motioning towards Aphrodite and Athena.

"Ew," I said, scooping up a huge plate of chilled shrimp, "Even me?"

"Well no, not you, "he continued, "Some of the nymphs are considered Zeus cousins, and Hera isn't related to him, which is good for us. Athena's mother was tricked into sleeping with him…but who wasn't. And Aphrodite…"

During Hermes' rambling, my eyes traveled back over to the table. Athena had Aphrodite pinned on the floor while she was twisting her hair and smiling. She nodded at me then gave Aphrodite a wet willy. It was hard to think that after thousands of years, we were just now realizing how broken we were. I shook my head as Aphrodite screamed out in disgust, then I turned my attention back to Hermes.

"She's a special one, isn't she…?" I said, licking the seafood sauce off of my finger.

I scooped up a large serving of pudding then grabbed an already filled goblet.

"So, you know we're related by father, not mother," Hermes continued, glaring at me.

"Yes I know…" I said.

He was silent as he looked at me with caution.

"Even if you weren't my sister, I wouldn't defile your body. Why is it so hard for everyone else to…control themselves?"

"Most of us are bastard children!" I hissed, "They're not really related…"

"That doesn't mean we should act like that!"

"So why did you sleep with Aphrodite countless times?!" I yelled.

The clutter and chatter of the room fell silent as everyone turned their heads to us. I waved to assure everything was fine and looked back at Hermes. This was a typical conversation. And sadly all of my siblings had slept with the other except for me and Hermes, and Apollo and I.

Athena had been tricked by Apollo who was under a love spell that Eros had purposely placed on him so Athena would conceive a grandchild for my father. When everything was done, Apollo spilled his seed, and begged Athena to pretend she was with child.

When the entire thing fell through, Zeus asked that Apollo be cursed with unfathomable knowledge, since he beguiled him. Ever since then, all Apollo does is tell people things they don't care to hear! But I figure if he put his powers to use on humans who clearly don't have a clue, he'd find his curse more useful.

After coming out of my trance, I could feel Hermes staring at me, but the tension hadn't changed. I put my plate down to rub his back. Then I took a sip of wine.

"Everything bad that's ever happened is all on Zeus," he said, darting his glare at our father.

"He's nothing of the sort…" I said softly.

"And he calls his self a *god*."

I placed my hand over his mouth as our father started to walk by. He raised an eyebrow at us as he walked to take his seat next to Io, who was still had her nose twisted up. If Hermes voiced the slightest doubt in my father, he would be cast out of Olympus. My hand left his face, and I became uneasy with the steadying silence that began to envelope the room.

Zeus stood, clinking his silverware against his goblet. Everyone hushed instantly, and he smiled nodding in every direction of the table.

"We need to address a certain matter," he said, still looking around, "Another one of our kind, my child, has been marked for treacherous murder over thousands of years. And an Archangel of Death has been hired to assassinate this goddess."

Everyone gasped dramatically, and I watched my mother slowly rise out of her seat and walk in my direction. The hairs on the back of my neck came to attention as I began to remember the dream. I attempted to focus my attention on my father, but I felt irresolute.

"It is our duty to convince him otherwise. The crimes this goddess is being charged for were not committed by her hand. So deception lies in the house of the gods," Zeus continued.

At this point, I was holding my stomach. Those were the very words the Teiresias spoke when he came. I turned and headed towards the door since there was nothing more I could bare to hear. Hera, as I presumed, hastened quickly after me, literally two steps behind. As soon as I reached my father's study, she whisked me around by my shoulder.

We searched each other's eyes heedlessly as she leaned in to hug me. I was never an affectionate person, but I lapped my chin on her shoulder.

"How does he know," I sobbed quietly, "And why is he after me?"

Hera didn't say much, but she continued to rub my back as if she were searching for the right response.

"If your father ever admitted anything he did, chaos would break lose. Do you realize that?" she asked.

"Yes…but…"

"If everything is true, then I'm sure explaining to him…"

I pushed my mother off of me, and stared at her in shock. Ignoring the tears pouring down, I ran out of compound to the steps and sat down. Why am I being accused of something I've never done? And how come my father wouldn't protect me? Surely Teiresias didn't mean my father wasn't going to save my life?

I sobbed at the thought of his words. As my tears slowly began to subside, I hugged my stomach and rocked a little. Apollo shuffled to sit down, blankly staring at me. He was just as emotionless as I was. He hesitantly placed his hand on my back while looking off into the distance.

"He can't get away with it this time. He has blatantly fed you to the dogs," Apollo said softly, "It's almost as if he were slowly eliminating each and every one of us."

I couldn't respond without insulting my father. I nodded at Apollo then looked out into the distance as well.

"Chances are this Angel will investigate. They are given a time limit for their victims. So it's not like you'll die when you return to Earth."

"That's it!" I said, suddenly excited, "I'll stay here! Apollo, you're a genius!"

"You can't stay here either. If he's after your life, you'll jeopardize all of us," he said, giving me a sad look.

I settled my emotions at his reaction. He was more than likely right.

He helped me walk down the stairs, and then waited for my chariot to arrive. Once I was seated inside, I waved good bye, and directed the charioteer to my temple. I was surprised to find all of the candles were lit, and the pool of water was still emitting a fountain.

In fact, I found it strange. I made my way to my room when I noticed that burned parchment I left on my kitchen counter was neatly placed on my bed. I rolled my eyes and knew instantly who had laid it there. Before retreating to my front room, I grabbed a bag of coins for payment.

If only it were soap.

Clotho, Lachesis, and Atropos were clearly somewhere in my temple, *I could smell them.* I searched the front room, and found two of them perched in front of the rolling waterfall. Atropos stood first, but Clotho tripped her, then pushed past Lachesis. I had never had the pleasure of smelling such an awful stench. In fact, I was sure if the Angel didn't come for my life, their personal hygiene would surely do me in.

I stepped back a little and nodded at her, then sat down on my golden lounge. All three of the sisters smiled to each other then began chanting. Soon Lachesis was in a trance and she began to cackle before she spoke.

"Surely what Teiresias has told you will come to pass. You will die," she hissed.

Clotho popped her in the back on her head and caught the eyeball in midair. Everything disgusted me about them, but more so the eyeball. She adjusted it then looked at me as the eyeball twitched and moved out of control.

"There is a way to expose your father," she began, hoping I would feed into their trap.

"Lovely, I'll figure it out myself."

I threw the large sac of gold coins at the feet of Atropos, hoping this would make them leave. All three began to dig through the coins when Atropos shot up, slapped the eye out of Clotho's head, and stammered towards me. She came so close I could hear her skin decomposing.

"Either way, life will be lost. On either side or both. So chose your actions wisely," she said, running her finger down my cheek.

I was pinned down on my lounge with tears brimming at the edges of my lids.

"Thank you for your time," they hissed in unison.

A pattern of thick smoke swirled from their feet, then swallowed them in their departure. It was best I was alone. Me and my emotions were driving near chaos.

Even after a while I could still smell their rotten flesh in the room. I discarded my dress and slipped into the cascading water fall. Standing there, I allowed the water to pour down my head and over my body. I didn't care that I couldn't see, nor did I care if anyone walked in and saw me.

Sitting down, I crossed my legs and allowed my hair to flatten in the front of my face. I was weeping softly, but if anyone asked me, they wouldn't be able to tell. The Angel in my dream was the Archangel of Death. Crazy, right? You're in love with a being who's purpose is to kill.

And how strange was it that my name showed up in the crimes against heaven? I attempted to recall anytime I had wronged anyone, but all my thoughts linked to one individual.

My father...I gripped my ankles tightly, but shifted my position when I heard the wood from my lounge creek under someone's weight. I wiped my wet curls from over my left eye for a better view.

Apollo was laid out on my lounge eating an apple. He smiled gingerly and waved. I motioned for him to turn around. Like a child, he rolled his eyes, and turned his head as I stood to reached for a nearby towel .

After I secured it around my breasts, I walked over to him, and began to wring my hair out on his feet. He snapped his head around, forcing his body up the head rest. This tilted the lounge back. He fell over, and as his apple flew he cursed at me. I laughed at his pain, but fell silent when I noticed Aphrodite in the room as well.

"You're going to be killed for something you did not do," she whispered, walking over to me.

She handed me a sheer white robe with traces of flickering gold. As I unwrapped my towel, she looked down at my bare body and scoffed. This was the main reason Aphrodite and I clashed. She wasn't the most beautiful woman among the gods. She held herself in higher esteem than everyone.

Truth be told, Aphrodite was aging. Her eyes were always tired, even though her skin was flawless. She admitted a few hundred years ago that vanity kept her young. I guess her followers felt otherwise.

After I felt a little more comfortable, I sat on the floor in front of the fire place. Apollo fixed the lounge so Aphrodite could sit. I scooted back in between her legs and closed my eyes as she began to brush my hair. She was quiet but it was a relief that she was so gentle with what she was doing. It brought back memories growing up. How much she and Athena had looked after me, even then our family was battered and torn.

We were gods with amazing abilities. But for some reason, we didn't possess a drop of self-control or wisdom. Some of my brothers have raped Aphrodite, Athena, and

Medusa. Not just one or two but many. Pretending they cared, and then doing the same thing the previous person did. Did my father do or say anything?

Of course not.

He banished his oldest brothers to the pits of the bottom of the ocean to gain control of Olympus. Poseidon guarded their prison walls. But through my father's fits of rage, he drowned Poseidon. And for the babies that were born…the bastard children that were forgotten…he spited them with acts of neglect. So the people that amassed in worship slowly began to fade away.

Once she was done, she turned my head and cupped my cheeks. Tears were still producing from my languid eyes, and now I couldn't hold back my emotion. To my disillusion, Aphrodite was crying as well. It had been a long time since we had any kind of a connection. I felt as I did when I was a child hanging around her ankles, and my mother's. As much as I deprecated her purpose, I still loved her very much.

Apollo smiled, but all together seemed dispirited as he lingered by the ledge of my fireplace. It was obvious he was in deep thought as he paced backed in forth. His eyes met with mine as he drew closer to me.

"You need to beg for your life, and offer Zeus' in exchange. You cannot be killed for something you did not do," he said softly, placing his apple core at my feet.

"But he's an Angel. Summoned by God himself!" Aphrodite said in a hushed tone, "It's that Being's job!"

"She's being killed for…what I'm sure is something Zeus has done! Look at us!" he screamed at her, "Brothers and sisters do not share a bed. Brothers don't rape their sisters then kill the offspring. We are this way because of Zeus!"

Aphrodite was respiring heavily, still clutching the golden brush in her hand. She exaggerated her motions as she switched positions to stand. Looking at her, I could see her eyes had cleared, but she was still in bluster of feelings. I watched them anxiously, then stood up blocking Apollo from her view.

"I can't bargain for my life if it's my job to help a warlord…or an army. People die when my job is done right, so I am a murderer," I said, handing him his apple core.

"No…someone had to start the war in order for you to be able to do your job!" Apollo roared, chucking it to the floor.

He swept his hand over his dark curly hair, and then he rubbed his hand over his face.

"You need to find him before he finds you…then you need to address him in a matter to where he doesn't think you're coming on to him…as if he doesn't think you're lying, and give him some kind of evidence so he doesn't kill the wrong person…" Apollo mumbled.

"And have father killed instead?" I asked out of abashment.

"The only person who would miss him is Io…." Aphrodite said under her breath, "And even though our father would be dead…it wouldn't make a difference from the life he lived."

"He is not God. He is a super human that obtained unfathomable power and played with the gods lives, as well as the humans that worshipped him. He thinks he's high and mighty, but he's created his own mental hell…" Apollo said, walking to leave, "so it needs to be done."

Aphrodite followed behind him, her gesture in acquiesce as she left. And here I stood alone in a room swarming with warm air, but somehow managing to feel cold. How do you talk to someone on assignment, especially when their purpose is to eradicate? My only thought now was to find him before he found me, and beg for my life. But this was bothersome more so because I had a mental attraction to him.

You'd have to be a fool to be in love with the Angel of Death.

Chapter Four: Krythm

Entering the Realm of the Forgotten was like walking into a ghost hotel in Vegas. Every spirit that resided there had a gig. It was almost as if they solely came for one purpose-to seduce you into selling your soul. I only wanted the remains so I can finish the job I was given.

A breeze fluttered the covering over my nose and mouth as dust and ash swirled around, enshrouding me from head to toe. This didn't effect me, but the smell was unbearable. I gagged as I neared my destination. *Was this the fruits of my labor?*

Elmer's shop intertwined with a rotting corpse, which according to him was the first to die here. Because it was a super human, its flesh seemed to turn black over time. But its appearance was a trick of the eye. The dust, ash, and remains from most dying gods presented a dark purplish display. And unlike a human, it's flesh took centuries to decay.

Since there was a risk for their spirit hosting in a mortal's body, all dying deities were commanded to perish here. If not here, they were ordered to take krythm. *Ya…right…*Obviously, since none of them listen, I came here for the poison to finish my assignments *without a trace.*

Which is another reason why I despised my purpose.

It was Elmer's job to insure they wouldn't escape if they were sent here, and it was his responsibility to distribute what I valued so much…*krythm*. It was extremely effective when it was concentrated. You only needed a little bit, and it was wise to turn it into this form. This allows for a speedy disposal.

I walked into Elmer's messy shop. He's broken record playing skipped beats here and there as it droned to a score by Chopin. He mumbled to his self as he looked over a molded trap of papers on his desk. Once he saw me, he grinned from ear to ear and stood up straight. Then he clapped his decomposing hands together, and began to walk in my direction. Since the creation of super beings, Elmer was the overseer of this realm.

"I thought you did away with him in a clean manner. No one knew a thing. Besides that city is crazy anyway, what were they going to say?" he said, cackling and smiling, "what can I do for you?"

"I need a concentrated form of krythm. I have a goddess from Olympus I'm after this time," I said, attempting to sound serious.

Elmer stopped walking towards me with his smile fading. He seemed disturbed with my announcement, but it was a part of his curse to help. He nodded then arbitrated his movements over to a broken filing cabinet.

The drawer he opened appeared to be the only one that was in working order. Elmer reached his bony decaying fingers into it, and drew out two pearl shaped pills, no larger than the size of a fish egg. Then he reached into his back pocket, and pulled out a silver capsule. After that he closed the lid and handed it to me then grabbed my wrist.

Elmer's flesh was cold and dank, and his grip was stronger than I anticipated. I grimaced at his action but I was ready to hear what he had to say.

"I want you to consider other options besides killing this woman," he hissed, "she comes from a family of dogs."

"If it's her I'm to kill, than it's her that will be killed," I answered back, trying to remain calm.

He loosened his grip and meandered away from me. Once he was behind his desk, he shuffled through the papers on top until he found what he was looking for. There sat two very large scrolls that took up most of the space on his broken desk. He dusted them off then stared down briefly.

"I cannot direct you to where you need to read, but these are the *Accounts of Actions* of deities from Olympus…in relation to Zeus. ……"

"Wait, *the* god of Olympus?" I said, suddenly confused, "what does that have to do with her?"

"About ninety percent of all deities are either related to Zeus, have been impregnated by Zeus, or have been killed or tricked by Zeus…"

"Yes but her name came up in the reports, not his…"

"I wonder why…" he said in a grim manner, "famously eradicating, but always chimerical…Zeus."

"It isn't my place to ask," I said, showing my doubt.

He knitted his dark grey brows together at my response.

"So consider this," he said, shoving the scrolls into my arms, "before you kill an innocent being."

As the Archangel of Death, I could never question my purpose. So I wasn't sure if I wanted to read the scrolls Elmer gave me. I began to walk to the edge of the realm, and nodded at Theros, the gate keeper. The last time I had been here, he was missing an ear. Now most of his face was gone, including both of his eyes. But he somehow managed to nod every time.

I tucked the scrolls into my bag, with my wings in prolongation. Before I considered descending I looked back at Elmer once more. He was standing near a puddle of black water, smiling at me.

"And what happens when I find the truth!" I yelled back at him.

"I can't tell you that! I've helped you as much as I am allowed," he said, pointing to the heavens.

I frowned at his response, and floated upward. Then I spiraled diagonally to Earth as I began to aviate downwards. There usually wasn't enough time to think during a flight. Being that I had so much on my mind, I missed my landing. I circled around for a few more miles before reaching a safe landing point. And in an instant I was home.

As usual, my house was empty, even though I always felt like someone was watching me. I walked over to the living room window to see if my bird friend was outside in the tree. But today, he was sitting on the window sill, staring at me.

"Are you hungry?" I asked.

"No," I heard Nathan say.

I jumped, attempting to hide my reaction, and nodded at Nathan. Then I looked back, only to see the owl was gone. My emotions were clearly written across my face when I turned towards Nathan, who seemed uneasy and impatient as he watched me walk back into my kitchen.

"Are you always watching me now?" I asked, pouring out the rest of my juice.

I noticed it filled barely a quarter of my glass and I wondered how long Nathan had been here.

"I can buy more," he said, watching my disappointment, "What took so long today?"

"Elmer says I need to investigate more," I said, gesturing to my bag.

Nathan carefully removed the scrolls, then placed them next to his arm and smiled.

"Do you know what this is?" he asked, sounding excited.

"No…" I answered, showing how much I didn't care.

"This is a list of angels, deities, and demigods. Their relations, crimes, powers, deaths, parents, all that. The *Accounts of Actions*."

Now I was interested.

"Angels have parents?" I said, purposely oblivious.

"Of course we do. We don't know who they are because…" he started off.

His smile slowly disappeared as he realized he was taking his curiosity too far. But the question I had was the relation between Zeus and this goddess, Enyo. I reached for the scrolls and opened up the first one. To my disappointment, everything was written in Ancient Greek. I slammed my hand down, and pulled the hair in my face back.

"Do you know Ancient Greek?" I asked Nathan.

"No, but my adoptive mother does."

"Ya Ya?" I asked, even more confused.

He nodded as he pulled an apple out of my fruit basket. I watched him devour it in silence. Nathan was always very quiet and introvert. He never laughed with anyone but me. He never hung out with anyone but me. And man, was he comfortable. He was always eating my food, sleeping on my bed, taking showers. I sometimes wondered if his mother was even alive.

"We need to pay her a visit then, a.s.a.p.," I said, gathering the scrolls back into my bag.

With the blink of an eye, we both began to ascend. Nathan had always been a little faster than me, but Nathan also landed anywhere. I found it strange that his mother lived in another state…but he was always at my house. Once we began to land, he motioned towards a broken down car garage near his house.

When my feet hit the ground, I realized a subtle tremor from Nathan's landing. He completely ignored what he had done, and began to stroll into his mother's house. I could hear the jubilation from her as she rounded the corner, asking if it was him.

He greeted Ya Ya sweetly, and bent over to kiss her cheek. Then he mumbled to her and pointed in my direction. Ya Ya smiled and stretched out her arms while she walked towards me. His mother was no taller than 4'11'', and since I was 6'4'', it was hard to hug her without feeling uncomfortable.

Soon we were seated at her counter, and she began to make us sandwiches. I pulled out the scrolls, and placed them out for her to see. She stopped and looked up at me smiling.

"Who is it you're looking for, A.Z?" she asked in a thick accent.

I blinked at the fact she knew what I was doing, then looked at Nathan in confusion.

"A goddess, Enyo. And her father…who I'm sure…but…"

"It's Zeus. She's one of his only children he had while married."

"That can't be accurate," I said in frustration.

"It is," she said, opening one scroll.

Nathan began to grin once she started chanting, and soon the scroll was illuminated with a golden light. Ya Ya beamed as well once she was done, and then she spoke into the scroll. I had never seen anything like this in my life, and Nathan was amused with my reaction.

She turned the scroll to face me, and pointed to Enyo. I could see her as clear as day, stuffing her dark brown curls into the hood of a coat. Then I could see where her current location. From the décor of the room, it appeared to be a temple. And a temple would be in only one place-Olympus.

I started to take mental notes of everything I could view when I noticed a tall male taking both of her hands and speaking to her. Curious as to what he was saying, I moved my face closer when the image disappeared. Soon a list of names began to appear on the page, followed by branching and separation.

From what I could make out, it was a family tree, but I did not see Enyo's name appear. Puzzled and feeling defeated, I fixed my gaze back on Ya Ya. She pushed a sandwich to me and Nathan, then looked sighed.

"Her name hasn't been taken out of history, but it seems to be that way so you could not find her," she explained, watching my reaction as well, "But I insure you Zeus is her father."

"That still doesn't mean anything to me," I said, convinced she was the one I needed to kill, "She's the goddess of war."

"Well, I suggest you do a little research," Ya Ya said, rolling the scroll back up.

"The picture?" I asked, confused again.

"Ah, the scroll was given to you for your assignment. At some point or another, her name was said near it or around it. It has a form of intelligence even a smart phone cannot comprehend. So it knows the nature of your job."

"Or it's a trick," Nathan said, scooting my sandwich towards him.

I smacked his hand, then popped him in the back of his head. He shoved me softly, then turned his attention on his mother. I saw how she looked at him, and I began to wonder if she knew he was an Angel.

It was something I had always pondered about him. Here I was, sent from heaven to work. And here he was, with a mother. They laughed for a moment, then Ya Ya became attentive to me again.

"Why is it you're searching so deeply for her?"

"Research for personal knowledge," Nathan answered for me.

His eyes shone mischievously when I looked his way. No, she didn't know either of us were Heavenly Beings. As curious as her ignorance was, I was more bothered she chanted in order to make the scrolls illuminate to her will.

I smiled at Ya Ya, then took a bite of my sandwich. I either did my job, or I didn't. If for some reason I couldn't, there was no such thing as a legitimate reason. As soon as it was discovered, I became a fallen angel.

It doesn't seem so bad if you don't know what's in store. It's by far the most painful thing an angel can experience-so I've heard. While some angels have been cast into the pits of hell, others are sent to Earth to live out their days.

Wasting away can take up to hundreds of thousands of years. Most fallen angels remain hidden, because the idea of living life on earth is torture itself. Loving someone and watching them die. Never really being able to have children. Not being able to keep friends….

I started to wonder about Enyo now, and if she were truly innocent. The only way I'd be able to find out anything else is if I talked to her. And how would that go? I saw her at the super market, and continued to think about her. Her shape, those lips, the way she walked…

Nathan pressed his hand against my shoulder and looked into my eyes.

"By the way, I should tell you, that owl is always there when I arrive. And I've learned from my mother, that an owl means Hermes has a message for you."

"Hermes? Who the heck is Hermes?" I asked.

"Messenger for the gods," Ya Ya said softly.

I scoffed for a moment, then thought about it. Perhaps I should talk to the owl, instead of offering it food. Nathan figured out what I was thinking, and packed the scrolls back into my bag.

"Is there anything else the scrolls are for?" I said, completely forgetting everything Elmer and Nathan had told me.

"Yes, they give a list of crimes committed. It doesn't matter what. War treason. Murder. Adultery. It's in there. You'll find a lot of it is connected to, or associated with Zeus. But don't be fooled. It was written like that to present a clean image to his followers if one ever retrieved these scrolls," Ya Ya answered

"So…he's basically an asshole and he wants no one to know," I asked, slightly amused, "he sounds like a *real* stand up guy."

"One of his mistresses actually betrayed him, which I find very interesting. He just so happens to favor her the most. You can seek her council as well if you wish," she said sweetly, "she goes by Io."

I nodded at the advice, nodded at Nathan, then ascended. The flight to my house seemed to take longer than the flight to Nathan's. Then I realized I was trying to keep up with him. Once I landed, the owl was again perched on the window sill. I walked over to it, then nodded.

"I don't know how to summon you to human form, but its best you don't do it outside…"

A bright flash of light started up in my kitchen, and there appeared a curly haired, fair skinned man. My fire alarm weakly peeped after his arrival. I surveyed him a little. He seemed to be glowing, but his face was downcast. I assumed his haberdashery on him would be a chiton, with an olive leaf tucked behind each ear. Surprisingly, he was dressed as an average Joe.

He took a deep breath, then he walked over to me. He sighed once more, then stuck his hand out for me to shake it. I laughed at his composure, then shook back. Feeling out of place, I sat down on my couch, and turned the TV on.

"This is not happening," I said, pretending to be interested in a horrible commercial.

"But it is…and I'm not hungry, by the way…" he said, almost in a feminine manner.

For some reason, I felt uncomfortable when he sat down so I scooted over, giving him a generous amount of room. He looked directly at me, then took a deep breath again.

"Does it stink?" I asked, irritated with his behavior.

"I'm Enyo's brother," he said, ignoring my question.

"Oh? By what relation?" I asked.

"We have the same father…"

"Lemme take a wild guess, Zeus?"

"You don't seem enamored by this information. But I did come to plead for her life…"

It was clear that no one felt Enyo deserved to die for the crimes she had committed. Annoyed with his request, I stood up to walk to the fridge, when I remembered my juice needed to be replaced.

"Let's go for a walk," I said, grabbing my jacket.

He followed me out of my front door, and stayed silent for a few blocks. When I turned to speak to him, he ran into my chest. His small frame bounced off of me, and he fell onto the pavement. Hermes stood up, and dusted *the front* of his pants off, then he shoved his hands into his pockets.

"How are you sure Enyo didn't do anything?" I asked, looking down at him.

He peered up with his bright blue eyes, and smiled.

"She's for diplomacy, not dictatorship."

"Yea…you're a messenger," I said, watching my breath swirl into the night breeze.

"She only helps the side that isn't in the wrong, Azreal," he chirped.

The fact that he knew my name stung. Then I thought…I had been killing his kind for thousands of years. The idea of having that kind of a reputation with a god rubbed me the wrong way. I stiffened my stance, and shoved my hands into my pockets as well.

"Nothing is going to convince me," I said, turning to walk again.

"We know, but I'm sure you'll make the right choice. I am not the god of persuasion. I'm just my father's messenger. So I have little use…" he said sadly.

"Who is we? And you're not as much of a threat to him as your siblings are."

He nodded at my response, then continued to walk beside me. Once we made it to my job, and I nodded at Patricia who was smoking a cigarette outside. Then I made my way to the breakfast aisle, and picked up a jug of juice. Hermes took it out of my hands, then headed to the front to pay. He nodded at the cashier, but didn't pull out any money.

Darting past, I saw Hermes walking towards the women's bathroom. As I passed the cashier, I noticed his eyes were bright blue as well. Confused as usual, I followed behind Hermes. Once I apprehended him, a bright light came from the crack of the door. Then Enyo popped out, looking bewildered.

"I couldn't find him there," she said, panicking, "Elmer said he had already collected the krythm, and made his way back to-"

She caught me staring at her, then she glared at Hermes. He seemed uneasy for a moment, but he kept his stance. The cashier came up behind pushing all of us to the equipment room. Once we were inside, he closed and locked the door, then turned a light on. Enyo was still staring at me as if she had never seen an angel, but she was also interested in the cashier.

"Apollo!" she hissed, pushing away from him, and running into me, "why are you guys here?"

"To plead your case," I answered, catching on to everything, "I'm sorry but it's my job…"

"You have to read the scrolls…" Apollo said, walking to me, "It will give you the answer you seek, instead of the hearsay you're receiving."

"Look…"

I stopped just to pulled the juice from Hermes hands, then I turned my attention to Apollo.

"You don't understand," Apollo continued, "our father would never openly take the blame for all the wrong he has done. It's easier for him to live like this if someone else takes the blame….whether it's his child or not….You have to read those scrolls…"

"It's my job, I can't just go…hmmm…well…she's pretty and doesn't seem like she'd do this so…." I tried to explain, "I'll become a fallen angel. Do you realize that?"

No one counterattacked my response. Instead they exchanged glances. I opened the door, and bolted to the back of the store. Whenever I was upset, I usually tried to fly. But I was intercepted by Enyo. She had to have been right behind me when I ran out of the room. She grabbed my shoulder to turn me around. She was looking fiercely into my eyes as if she was searching for something.

I sat my juice down by the sink and waited for Enyo to please with me again.

"I know this is your job, but my life is in danger," she said, trying to get through to me, "you'll be killing me for things my father has done!"

I could sense she was close to tears, though her animosity towards her father was sickening. How deranged would you have to be to hope for the death of a loved one? She was quivering a little, with her nerves getting the best of her. Enyo shuddered, blinking back tears before she spoke.

"I know it seems crazy, but I wouldn't kill someone just to get my way. Please have sanctity here, you know how gods and goddesses are. I am not like-"

"Do I know you?" I said, cutting her off, "Can you be exalted in my heart? I'm not sacrificing what's right because you may be missed!"

Forgetting my juice again, I pushed through to the back room, then swung the large steel door open as I prepared to take off. Without regards to the fact that she was watching me, I unveiled my wings, and soared off into flight. I looked back for a moment and saw her watching me as I flew away.

She had to have known I marveled her; she was breath taking.

How did heaven feel about that?

Chapter Five: Imperceivable Desire

Azreal was even more beautiful than I had dreamed him to be. But he had a very bad temper, and he seemed extremely impatient. I watched him as far as I could, then I turned to walk back into the store. Hermes had vanished, and Apollo took his spot in the front scanning merchandise. He nodded slowly at me, seeming a bit somber once I began to exit.

I felt I could not get through to him. But I had to make my way to his house to talk. Even if it meant he would kill me. As I walked…it hit me. He had the perfect chance to do so, and he didn't. *Twice* this Angel had the opportunity to kill me, and twice he ran away! That there made me feel there was a possible attraction.

I ran up the street and stopped on his block. Looking into the night sky, I could see him descending into the middle house. Then I ran up to where he lived and slowly walked to the door. I paused as I listened, then I jiggled the door knob. I tried to listen again, when I felt a hand grab my shoulder. I jumped in fear, but held my tongue.

Turning, I could see Azreal glaring at me. Then he opened his door, and shoved me into the entry way. He flicked on a light while pushing me into his kitchen, where the *Accounts of Actions* could be seen sitting on the counter.

"Sit," he said, pointing to a stool.

I did so, nervously, and watched him open his fridge then slam it shut.

He cursed a little as he ran a hand through his black curls. Then he pressed both of them on the counter, and continued to glare at me.

"You realize that it's you I have to kill, and even if I did kill your father…what difference would it make?" he asked me, assembling his previous face, "even if you are a woman…"

He softened his glaring look briefly to examine me, but arbitrated his facial expression. I was clearly a physical hindrance. He had taken the time…

"Surely there's some way other of convincing…" I said, breaking our connection.

"Right," he scoffed, now looking for a glass.

Azrael ran the faucet in hesitation. Once his glass was filled, he took a swig and made a face, then sat it on the counter. Even with my life being in peril, I couldn't help but to gaze upon him. This Being was an awe-inspiring, heart enchanting, mindful alluring handsome…distraction.

Azrael was tall, with very broad shoulders. His attributes included a head full of thick, black curly hair, and beautiful blue eyes…accompanied by full lips…And from what I could see, he had a very nice physique. I cascaded my eyes down his arms to his hands, which were still firmly planted on his counter. He caught me watching him and tried to seem menacing.

"They know you're here. So now I want proof that you are Zeus' daughter. Then I have to make a decision of what to do. Whatever your story is, and the clarity of your information is based on if you or your father dies. Or both."

"As long as he's punished, my life is not a concern," I said, still surprised with my attraction to him.

I grabbed the scrolls, and spread out the second. Placing my hand in the middle, I closed my eyes and began to chant. Once I opened them, a list of names began to appear as they sorted out into branches and subdivisions. I sited my father's kin and found my name near the top of the family tree. Azrael looked down at it, then at me in confusion.

"Earlier…" he sputtered.

"Because this scroll has a power of intelligence. No one wants me dead but you and heaven. So it hid my name. It's simple though. It knows the honest, and dishonest. The hurt and the love. It's almost like a child, really. An intelligent, tell all child."

Azrael seemed displeased with this, as he looked skeptical. Just as soon as I opened my mouth to counter an answer, another angel appeared in the kitchen next to him. The house shook violently with his arrival and he peered down on me in disgust. He then shot his gaze at Azreal, who was glaring right back at him.

"I told you, they know you're here..." Azrael said softly.

"It has to be proven that she is in fact a child of Zeus, through marriage and not the intercepts of a good time, and, it has to be proven that Zeus is the murderer! Otherwise, don't bother!" he roared at Azreal.

I was afraid Azrael he would lose his temper. He hands were still pressed against the marble counter, and his lips were tightly pierced together. He turned to the other angel, who was even tall than him. Perhaps I had a thing for Angels; this one was rather attractive as well. He had long, straight black hair, and luminous grey eyes. As fearful as I was, I couldn't help but to stare at the both of them.

Azrael looked to this Being, then to me and shook his head slightly. I coughed, then looked down, hoping he didn't notice. Azrael took a deep breath, and began to speak.

"How do I prove she's the daughter of Zeus, and how do I prove he's the guilty one?"

"You obviously need to make a trip to Olympus and investigate. However, the time span in which you have to complete this job still stands at 30 days...." Zerachiel spoke.

His voice boomed still, vibrating everything around. Since it began to make my ears ring, I attempted to cover them and continued to watch the conversation.

"And you," he roared, barely opening his mouth, "I have no idea what gave you the sense of coming here, but it's best you keep your distance. Because if he doesn't kill you, I will."

"That isn't your job, Zerachiel," Azreal snipped.

"Well, she needs to know her place. So. Do as you've been instructed, and I advise you not to teleport. A spiritual transference is the last thing we need..." Zerachiel said, turning to face me, "if it really was your father, I want you to consider that no matter what he's done to you, he gave you life. So rather than being joyous someone else is taking the blame, you should feel grief that he's sick enough to do all that he's done."

I got the feeling that this angel felt he had to be right all of the time. And regardless of how right he was at the moment, he made it his business to make me feel like shit. I nodded at him, but did not look up. When he ascended, the house shook violently again, and it was just Azreal and I. *Crying in front of him would probably piss him off.*

Azreal looked at me without expression. Then he rolled up the scrolls, and stuffed them into a bag sitting on the counter.

"We have to enter it like I would do any other realm," he said.

I was completely astonished that he allowed this angel to talk to him in that manner...And yet he was as calm as ever.

" Wait....what? I don't fly. I can't..." I said, sputtering a little.

We blinked at each other momentarily before Azreal spoke again.

"I've got that covered, but I can't catch you if you fall..."

I reached out to grab his hand, but drew back and looked at him. He was smirking ever so slightly and still motioning for my hand.

"I guess your job would be done then, right?" I said, peering up at him.

"The point was, don't let go."

I nodded then with apprehension, took his hand. He embraced my waist tightly, and motioned for me to wrap my arms around his neck as well. Drawling out my motions, I attempted not to stare into those intense blue eyes. Then Azrael took a deep breath while looking down.

"I don't typically do this, so please tell me if I'm going too fast. And for heaven's sake, don't puke on me…"

I laughed at his request then nodded. My nerves were getting the best of me, but I was curious as to how we would fly through his ceiling without busting it open and damaging it.

His wings began to proliferate slowly as they did before, and he flapped them a few times. I could feel the strain in the back of his neck as a few stray feathers floated around the light in the kitchen.

Then Azrael looked down at me again. In an instant we were airborne, and the feeling left me debilitated. The air rushing by us didn't affect me as I thought it would. The blur of scenery I expected was the complete opposite.

When he was high enough I could see the city. When that was out of view, I caught a glimpse of the country. Once we hit the first layers of the atmosphere, I saw how it began to mold into the world. And in the twinkling of an eye the planet began to appear.

Maybe it was how fast we were going, and the thought of being noticed that scared me. Soon we were out of the atmosphere, passing the Realm of the Forgotten. It didn't take as long as I assumed, and Olympus wasn't a far stretch thereafter.

He began to spin once he hit Olympus' atmosphere, then he spiraled to a smooth halt while still in midair. I was clutching the back of his neck, my nails digging into his flesh. My heart was still racing, and my wind whipped face burned a little.

He landed softly, then let me down. I gazed up at him once more as he gathered those beautifully crafted wings back. As we stood there, I gawked in wonder at them, as I was ever so curious to touch his retreating beauties. But he stopped me as I drew closer, and handed me the scrolls. Disappointed, I took them and grabbed his hand to lead the way.

"It's late here," I said, walking to a post to wait for a chariot, "so maybe we can do some research in the morning. I have a place you can sleep-"

"I don't sleep," he whispered, wiggling out of my grasp, "but I take it you do."

"Not lately," I said sadly.

Azrael acknowledged the tone in my voice, and looked up once my chariot had arrived. He helped me into it, then took his place next to me. I was enamored by the sheer strength of him, and how delicate he could be. I caught myself studying this magnificent Being again, and turned to watch the temples we passed.

"Is that Aphrodite?" he asked, gawking at my sister.

"Yes," I said, disgusted by her.

He watched in abhorrence as well. She was giving all of Olympus the usual show of her sexual acts, and I just so happen to have him with me. I sneered as she moaned loudly, almost as if she knew we could see her. As the chariot road along, I was bothered that the further we got away, the louder she became. By the time we reached my temple, I was extremely annoyed, and almost introvert. Since Azrael was with me, I had to pretend it didn't bother me.

"Our only issue is that any wrong my father has ever done may only be in the Book of the Lost-it's the only source that proves it. That's in the library of Hades. And as you can imagine, we have to bribe our way to get it without losing ourselves."

Azrael nodded as we passed the room with my waterfall. He stopped for a moment to admire each and every chamber we passed until we were in my study. Then he took a seat behind my desk and rested his huge feet on it. He placed both of his hands behind his head, and smiled as if he was pleased with himself.

"I've always wanted to do this," he said, smiling like a child, "I'm sorry it had to be your desk."

"I'm sorry you're not all about business like I thought."

"I'm sorry your sister was having obnoxious sex on our way here…" he retorted.

"Me too," I said under my breath.

"No wonder…"

"No wonder what?" I said, ready to fight.

"No one worships gods anymore. If that's what they're really like..."

Since I didn't have a response, I shooed him out of my chair, and sat down. Then I rolled out the first scroll, and placed my hand in the middle. He stood over me and watched as it lit up with names.

"The first scroll is specifically designed to note events such as wars, courtships, and murders….Search," I said softly, "Zeus, Enyo."

It began to trace it's memory like a computer scanned its files. Then it stopped over a vast section of font.

"History of crimes," I said, watching the docket.

Azrael wowed as he moved a little closer. I had to admit, this was better than your average android powered tablet.

"Between what times," I read out loud to myself, "100 B.C. To 300 A.D."

"That's a long time…" Azrael whispered.

The list was astonishing. Unlike anything I expected, and far greater than I imagined.

"Wars," I asked as clear as I could.

As it scanned I noted that Azrael was watching me still. This time he was examining me, as he did when I had first met him. He seemed pleased with what he saw, then he started to look around my room. When I looked back, I noticed there were divisions, and subdivisions of wars in the time periods I had asked for. As I began to read, I thought back on some of the wars I had helped with. It was great that this scroll showed disputes started by Zeus, *but not why.*

Disappointed with my find, I rolled the scroll shut and looked at Azrael. He was playing with my bow and arrow, pointing it towards my window. He knew I was watching him, but instead he let the arrow go. I watched in shock as it flew out of my office, and into my bedroom. Then it soared out of the window, and most likely into someone.

"That was a gift!" I squealed, trying to pull it from him.

"From?"

I fell silent at his question, then turned my head away as I sat my bow down.

"So it isn't a gift. It's like a 'Thanks for taking the fall' kind of thing," he said.

"Like the building of this temple was," I said, walking out.

I grabbed his hand again, then guided him to my guest room. I noticed how small the bed was as I looked over his frame.

"Maybe you can sleep in my bed?" I said, smiling a little.

His movements became rigid, but he smiled too and nodded.

"Yes, because that's not a bed. That's a pillow," he said teasingly.

I chuckled a little, then guided him back to my room. He twisted his hand out of my grasp before reaching my door and stopped me by the shoulder.

"Stop grabbing my hand," he said softly, "it doesn't bother me like it should, but I'm sure Zerachiel, and everyone else in heaven feels like you're up to something."

"Oh ya?" I scoffed, "it sounds like you think I want you. I'm sure all of the human broads down on Earth can't get enough of you, but I have standards…"

"And *WHAT* could be higher than an Angel?!" he proclaimed boldly.

"A god!" I roared.

"Have you seen your kind!?" he roared back, rearing his self to my face.

For a moment it seemed as if he wanted to kiss me, and unknowingly, my lips parted as well. But instead I pretended I wasn't attracted to him in any way, and I stepped back to continue arguing.

"Well, at least I live for myself!" I screamed at him.

"I am doing what I was created to do. You're doing whatever your father has instructed you to do, and that was to clean up his messes!" he roared back at me, "So I may be a monotone, rule follower, but at least my purpose isn't for someone's selfishness!"

I couldn't say anything back. And no matter how mad it made me, he was right. Azreal came from God. Pure, holy, righteous. I came from a patchy marriage condoned by my father in order to gain a better reputation from the humans worshipping him – I wasn't really supposed to be here. Azreal noted my reaction, and sped past me into my room. Then he sat on my bed, placing his hands on his face.

"Good night," he said mumbled.

"I thought angels don't sleep?" I asked, hoping he knew I was mocking him.

"They do, I don't," he mumbled again.

"Why?" I asked again.

Azrael lifted his head out of his palms just to glare at me. His expression reeked of invoked aggravation. In fact, I became uneasy.

"At least your purpose is a purpose."

I knew what I said wouldn't fix the argument we had, but I wanted him to know it was greater to be crafted in the image of God, than in the desires of a fallen deity. As I made my way to the guest room, I felt my tears beginning to spill from my eyes. And by the time I laid down, I was engulfed in sorrow. It wasn't because my life was on the line. It was what we would soon discover about my father.

And the fact that I was in love with Azreal.

Chapter Six: An Immortal's Idealisms

Soon I could hear Enyo snoring softly. It didn't matter since I couldn't sleep. And I was almost unsure of walking around her temple. She was positive we would find what we were looking for and that everything would be alright.

What if she discovered something that made everything worse? She would lose her father, and realize her purpose was only to please his selfish acts his whole entire life. Or what if he found out I was here, and decided to have her killed regardless, where would that place me?

It is something I didn't want to think about. Since I could tell she was emotional towards me, it was strange to think that I was towards her as well. It's unfortunate this is happening…she's a goddess and I'm an Angel. And unless I was absolutely sure she was worth me losing my place in heaven, I won't bother.

The idea of being happy with her started to make a place in my heart and my mind, and it seemed like it began to manifest. There was something about Enyo that captured my special attention. But I had a job to do. The hard part now? Doing the job right, and forgetting that I ever met her.

I turned on my side and noticed someone sitting in the chair next to my bed. I sat up and scooted back a little, trying to reach the lamp.

"My name is Apollo, Azreal," he said softly, "I have a bit of advice for you."

I clicked the light on, giving him a strained look.

"Okay," I said hesitantly, recalling his face from the supermarket.

"Do your job, and just that. Because I can assure you, if you think you'll fall in love and be okay, you have another thing coming.…" he started off, turning on the taller lamp sitting next to him.

"Who said…" I asked, showing my bemusement. This was becoming a trend.

"Eros, god of love, is her brother as well. He mentioned he felt there was a strong connection between the two of you, which now makes me question her motive in bringing you here," Apollo answered.

"Trust me, whatever is there won't be sought after," I said, trying to explain.

I'm such a liar…

"Why?" he asked, looking puzzled as well.

"I am not to mingle with humans, or other immortals. It's a sin. I could only be with her if I lost my place in heaven. But I'm not willing to disobey God because she has a crush on me."

Apollo nodded at my words, but I felt it wasn't convincing. He looked at me once more.

"Why are you here?"

"To do research on your father," I said under my breath, "This insures my job is done correctly."

"Spilled blood isn't enough in this line of work I take it. It has to be the right person?"

"Yes. Otherwise she'd be dead by now. Once someone says they're innocent, I have to investigate. But usually most state innocence to buy themselves time to run.…"

"You meant she should have been dead by now," he said, correcting me, "but something is stopping you?"

"Like I said. I'm under oath. Emotions aren't important right now…"

He nodded at my response as I felt the tension between us ease. Apollo stood to exit through the entry way. Then he stopped and turned to face me before leaving.

"I've never had the pleasure of meeting an angel, but I see what all the fuss is about. Good luck in all you do."

"I don't believe in luck," I answered quietly.

He waved, but did not acknowledge my riposte. I was beginning to see why most of the god's followers stopped worshipping them. There was a loss of civility, propriety, acknowledgement, and trust. It made me wonder what else Zeus had been up to outside of the murderous life he lead his daughter to live.

Since I had no intent of resting, I walked into her study and lit a few candles. I wasn't expecting much light. But soon it was bright enough from the ones glowing. I unrolled the first scroll, sat down, and pressed my hand in the middle of it as Enyo did.

I started to mumbled, unsure that chanting was the best idea. I also had no idea what Ya Ya or Enyo had been saying. To be frank, it sounded like indistinct…mumbling.

I jumped back a little as it illuminated and began scrolling titles. Without thought it lead right to Zeus' name, then pulled up his history. I opened my mouth to speak, but it started listing crimes against him. I again, became perplexed. Earlier she couldn't find anything on him, directly blaming him at least.

Right now, hundreds of thousands of crimes were being listed right before me. Then it stopped at a current enormity. My eyes widened at the details, and soon I was enraged and ready to find him. I rolled up the scroll and shot up from the chair when I noticed she was standing in her study.

Enyo smirked then gestured towards the scroll.

"If you found what you were looking for, you still have to prove it."

"How can I prove…anything? I know nothing about him."

"You stood up as if you were ready to do away with him. You should see the look in your eyes. It's straining, convinced," she said, walking a little closer, "What you need to know is in the Book of the Lost."

Trepidation was never an issue of mine, but this feeling had been etched into me since I've met Enyo. To a deity the situation was current, to a mortal it was centuries in the making. But the loss of life was greater than it should have been.

The pursuing side, the good guys to say the least, ended up surrendering. In an effort to stop future uprisings, the king of the losing army was behead…with his family included. Enyo knew how the battle went, but Enyo didn't know how the story ended or how it began. *So it was true.* She was to help with battle plans, and attack tactics.

I watched her study my face when I realized she had been admiring me again. I felt a little uneasy and scooted past her to sit on her bed.

"What did you find?"

"I'd rather not," I said under my breath.

"I beg you, tell me," she said, landing at my feet with her head down.

I was shocked at her action, and as much as I wanted to tilt her beautiful head up…

"It was like almost any war he started, why is what I found any different?" I said, clearing my throat.

"Because that scroll is emotionally intelligent. So whatever you were looking for, it showed you…exactly…"

"…It showed me…" I answered sternly.

She looked up at me as if she were hurt, but nodded, then stood. I grabbed her hand before she turned to leave as I pulled her close to me. Then I hugged around her waist and closed my eyes. *It felt so good to finally touch her, I had been thinking about her since I've met her…* She placed her hands on my head, and soon they were through my hair.

"I have to figure out what it is I need to do, but I give you my word, the right person will be put to justice."

Me, cooing words of judgment to a woman I could never love. An immersing feeling began to develop….

"Maybe you can throw him into prison with his other family members," she said, still running her fingers through my hair.

The sensation that lead me to continue my embrace became awkward when I thought about it.

I let go of her once I realized what I was doing, then I stood quickly and stared down at her in a weird manner. She noted my reaction and attempted to seem calm.

"We'll go to see Hades, and decided what to do after that. But that book is our only hope really," she stated.

"I wish…"I started to say. I cleared my throat and turned my back to her, "that what you say is true."

Since I began to feel comfortable around her, it meant my job would be even harder to complete. If for some reason we admitted we were in love, I would either have to erase her memory, or become a fallen angel. Neither was worth the strife, so I became adamant and started to make my way back into her study.

"How do we get to Hades?" I asked, tucking the scrolls into my bag.

"Simple. It's called the Underworld, but we also call it Media's Lair. There we pay the ferryboat slave, and I have the currency for our trip. After that it's all up to us not to be trapped there. You have an advantage. You can fly, and whatever powers your possess will still be with you. You are God-like in creation, and Hades couldn't do anything to you. Me on the other hand…"

"Bargain Zeus' position with him or better yet, his soul," I suggested, even more concerned about our future venture.

"It's an idea, and I think we may go with it..."

"Does every god here have a higher expectation of everything they hear?" I asked, showing that I was irritated.

"Yes."

"But you can't seem to meet the cry of simply acting…*right*."

"Angels fall too," she said snobbishly.

"Angels are given a purpose, and a choice," I said, growling a little, "I can choose to do right. I can choose to do wrong. But I don't have someone looking up to me either way!"

Enyo tilted her head back for a moment as her lips parting to fuss back. I didn't mean to hurt her feelings, but I felt I was under fire for not being a god. So we stood there in silence.   Impersonating apathy deemed a better option as I brushed past Enyo to the entrance of her temple.

"You're leaving without me," she said, keeping my pace.

"I'm sure I can find my way," I retorted, smirking at her inquiry.

Enyo stopped me by my shoulder then held up a finger. I watched her jog to the room, then jog back with a large messenger bag on her side. Then she smiled at me.

"Not all gods are assholes," Enyo quietly retorted, "and not all goddesses are stupid, selfish, slut drones."

Disregarding what she said, I turned to exit. Apologizing to her may allow her think that I was attempting to be with her. Or something….like that…It was bad enough I embraced Enyo as if I loved her. So it would be best to keep up our conversations about the task at hand.

"So how do we get there?" I asked.

"It's between the ends of the Earth, and the ends of this realm," she said, walking in front of me, "the only way for us to travel there is on foot. Or possibly horse back. But animals have a natural tendency to stay away from the Underworld."

"So then, what about a Pegasus, or a dragon…" I asked, attempting to mock her.

"A dragon? We aren't in Norway or Romania. And what do you know about dragons anyway, you're an Angel…"

"At one point they existed…"

"Look I know what you're getting at," she said, turning around and pointing me in my chest, "I get that. But I want you to know that you haven't been doing what you were supposed to have done. For instance, twice you had the chance to kill me and your job would have been done. But twice you didn't."

"I had received a warning, and a little advice before my run in with you…" I answered, getting annoyed.

"Is that what God told you?" she said, now mocking me.

"It's what I hear from Zerachiel. God doesn't have to talk to me if he doesn't want to. It is I who humbles myself before Him, not the other way around. And!" I said, cutting her off before she could speak, "I never question my purpose! Whether I'm in love with you or not!"

Enyo's lush, full lips turned upwards, revealing a child like smirk. But she then knitted her brows together in inquiry. Her eyes traveled from mine, then down she turned to keep walking. *I let it slip and it was now out of my control.* This had been the obvious reason I hadn't taken her life.

"The idea is not only to show humility, but to show self discipline," I said quietly.

"You're doing a great job," she answered with repugnance.

At that remark I fell silent. I walked with her until we were in the woods. Since I could not see Enyo I became a little nervous. So I flew up above the canopy and followed her until she stopped. As I landed I watched her assimilate a small lantern. She discarded the match and brought the light to my face.

"Azrael, you can't do that here unless you absolutely have to," she explained, starting to walk again.

"Why not?" I asked, still irritated.

"Because Angels that come here are usually hunted for sport," she said, turning to face me again, "and everyone knows why you're here. So it's best you keep it under wraps."

"Why would a *anyone* kill an angel?" I asked, showing I was antagonized.

"Because the gods are jealous of them."

Since this was obviously news to me, I began to question her motives as well. All of her brother's thoughts began to ring in my head as we continued to walk through the thickly branched forest. *Why had I allowed her to drag me here?*

After a few hours, I realized we began to make our way through shorter shrubbery. Then soon it was nothing but moss, rocks, and small streams. Enyo stopped to take a breath and stretched her arms. In the horizon I could see Earth almost as if it were a skip and a hop away. And like death on wings I could see the dimming light coming from the Realm of the Forgotten.

"Angels are killed because gods wish they could be like us?" I asked, trying to muster up a conversation.

"Yes. You have responsibilities, but you have always been more trusted," she answered, with her back towards me.

"Not always…" I added. I had a pretty good idea why Angels were targeted.

"I know, but…"

"Look, no one is perfect *but God*. If we all possessed the powers He did…with the selfish disdain we have on a daily basis…nothing would exist."

"I understand your anger towards us."

"Do you?" I challenged.

"Yes. Because we squander the powers we have."

I fell silent, but began to think of what should really be said. We both watched the horizon start to light up. There wasn't a sun, but a strange bright orange aurora began to skid across, swirling the clouds. In the blink of an eye a chariot wisped through the early morning sky then out of sight. From that, I could see the entrance to the underworld.

Finally, I took a deep breath, hoping the delivery of my story was enough for Enyo to understand.

"Before the world had been flooded, God had assigned 6 angels to help mankind survive off of the land. During their time on earth, they abused their authority by sleeping with the women that inhabited the world at that time. They mingled with the living creatures of God's creations as well, and failed to finish their tasks," I said, as we waited at the shore of a tar filled ocean.

Enyo looked at me, but quickly turned her attention to the boat nearing us. As soon as we boarded, I could sense she wanted to know more. I also figured I would have a hard time explaining the next part as well.

"Since angels have powers unlike humans do, mating with a female of course creates super beings…nephilims. The biggest issue with being a demigod is that when they die, their souls do not pass into heaven or hell. They either possess another body…Or as other cultures like to say, reincarnate another host…."

The pain stricken across her face caused me to stop speaking. She looked confused and showed her feelings had been hampered. Enyo rubbed her arms as if she were cold, and before we entered the oncoming darkness of a tunnel, she turned to me and looked up.

"We are mistakes," she whispered.

"Not God's, but…yes…"

"Well…no. He trusted them, and they failed Him…"

"You have been worshipped all these years from curiosity, fear, confusion, lies, and jealousy. You were never meant to exist," I said, trying not to sound too harsh.

"So what happened to them? I mean…those angels?" she asked, her face nearing mine so she could hear.

"They were banished, and sent to a special part of hell, specifically designed for them. They've been locked down there since…"

"Like the Titans…" she said.

I raised my eyebrow at her comparison, and continued to watch the tunnel as it twisted, and turned, nearing closer to the dim light in the distance. The moans of the dying could be heard. After all my years of executions, even this made my skin crawl. She tugged at my pants and pulled me to the middle of the vessel.

As we slowly moved through the passage way, I could see that familiar dark purple glow of a perishing god. The mist from the decaying dust swept onto the ship, and started a small fire. I nodded at Enyo's notion, but wiggled myself free from her grasp. It was becoming difficult to avoid her because she couldn't seem to not touch me.

"Angels are meant to help and protect. So when an Angel defiles a woman's body with their seed, they're going against the commandments of God," I said, hoping she would understand.

"Abusing their powers," she said.

"Yes…" I said, moving back slightly, "Even if you fall in love, you can never, ever…"

"So pretend you don't love me," she said.

It might be something I needed to do. I couldn't think of anything worse than losing my powers and becoming a fallen angel. *Well, losing her affection for some reason seemed to be an undeniable reason at the moment.*

I moved back a little more, then near the fire that was still burning. I walked over to be close enough to examine it, when I noticed something I hadn't thought of before. The day that I had met Enyo, there had been dark purple ash on the sink area in the back room. Although there had been trace amounts, it was noticeable, and odd to be found on Earth.

This trip seemed to be taking forever. Being that I had a billion other things on my mind, I felt that our request wouldn't be taken seriously. I also knew that Hades was known for having an underlining cause, even with the most simplistic things. With that thought, I endeavored to seem placid.

And there was Enyo, walking towards me to grab my hand. I snatched it back and glared down at her. I could feel her motive, and I almost felt too weak to fight back. Then, she grabbed the end of my shirt while pulling herself up to my mouth. I glared a little harder, but she seemed to enjoy the fact that I was also biting my lip. Enyo's parted slightly as she rose a little closer to retrieve a kiss, and as soon as I closed my eyes, a cold wind engulfed us.

"It's Manai, Hades right hand," she whispered, with both of her hands on my chest, "And he's a pompous prick"

"Azrael, aren't you sworn to purity?" Manai asked walking closer.

Enyo backed up darting a fierce look at him, then to me with concern.

"And goddesses are just about as filthy as their vanity," he hissed, surveying

Enyo.

"I need to speak with Hades," I said, trying to remain calm.

"I know. And you know…it's hard following you, I don't fly," he said in a taunting tone.

"What?" Enyo said out of confusion.

"What!" I growled, noticing how much my voice had changed.

"To make sure the job gets done…" he said, sneering.

"That isn't your place…" I said, stiffening my stance.

"Aren't you as bright as they come? It's obvious what Zerachiel said about you is true; you always see what's in front of you. But do you see it?"

A shocking revelation erupted into thought. The fact that he mentioned Zerachiel really got to me.

"Why would Zerachiel be here?" I asked quietly.

"Not exactly sure my friend," he said, patting my shoulder, "His issue is far more personal than either of you are willing to admit."

I frowned at his answer, and at the stench.

"I know!" he said, acknowledging my facial expression, "that's thousands of years of dying gods and goddesses. You might not know what real decay smells like. You only use small amounts. Imagine this….we like dead deity hoarders!"

He roared out in laughter, then began to walk off of the boat.

"Follow me please, and remind Enyo to keep her hands to herself. No one wants to fight."

She lunged at him, but I caught her by the wrist and turned her towards me.

"He may be helpful, even if he is what you said."

Enyo's skin was cold, and damp. And she was sweating not to mention she looked hysterical and weak. She fell into me for support, but I turned her back around and pushed her towards Manai.

"Stay focused," I implied.

The only beings that could withstand krythm were angels. Other gods were vulnerable, even if it happened to be just a little dust. And this place was filled with krythm.

With every chamber we passed you could see bodies piled on top of the other, some of which were still alive. And although their flesh just started to decay, a god's mind goes into limbo right before and during death. Mindless, and not yet dead. It had to be absolute hell.

We entered a chamber designed to be dust free, and sound proof. Even with being disgusted by everything we passed, I showed my concern about Enyo. Her breathing was labored, and she looked gaunt, as if she were aging.

Enyo slumped into the chair next to mine, and smiled. I placed my hand on her forehead, but before I could think Hades appeared in his chair. He wisped the smoked around him as it formed into a thick and weathered coat. Then he crossed his grey and purple stained hands out in front of him.

"Azrael, I never thought I'd meet you," he said greasily, cheesing.

"You and me both…"

"I know, most Angels think that. But most Angels don't fly here, either. And most don't make it out. It's a little treaty we have signed with Zerachiel…."

The hair stood up on the back of my neck from his name being mentioned again. But now, my curiosity got the best of me.

"What's you agreement with Zerachiel?"

"In this realm, he can't be watched or seen. No one can be. This is considered a pleasurable purgatory, actually. But back to your back stabbing guardian. He feels as if his boss isn't doing what needs to be done to rid the world of…people like me," he said smiling, "And although you are good at what you do, you're not perfect."

This news sounded deranged to me. But I attempted to remain emotionless as I hastened an answer.

"He's discontent with his position, but he has a higher ranking than me" I said, "…what does he get out of it?"

Hades smiled at me, and rubbed his hands together.

"His guardian displaced his trust in God, and as you were explaining to Enyo, he was cast out of heaven with 5 other angels. Zerachiel hasn't been the same since he witnessed that…"

I was in such disbelief at what I was hearing. Remembering how I told Enyo knowing certain things resulted in consequences, I wanted to forget all the laws I held an oath too. I could feel the anger rising in me as I listened to Hades continue with his story. As I began to drift into fury, I felt Enyo's cold hand on mine. She shook her head, and almost instantly I came back to.

"*If* you kill Zeus, he's got plans for this place."

"Zerachiel can't hold dominion over Olympus. God can't see this place because it isn't supposed to exist, but that doesn't mean he doesn't know what he's doing."

"Well, that's where you come in."

"Wuh…" I said, trying not to stammer, "Are you challenging my skills? Zeus will be killed, there's no doubt there."

"You have to *if you can*. You think I'm bad, you have no idea what Zeus has done…" he said, cackling again. He stood to walk around the large circular table.

Hades came to stand behind me and placed his hand on my chair.

"Zeus knows who God is, and he knows the most unforgivable sin. But Zeus is afraid to die. Because when he does, he has a special place just for him…" he said, moving over to Enyo's chair.

"That's impossible," I said under my breath.

"Oh, he isn't an original, he is a first descendant. But he isn't the only one remaining."

"The first descendants died off thousands of years ago…" I said in, sure of my knowledge.

"Or did they go into hiding, knowing their history with God, and mortals?"

It slowly began to dawn on me how long Olympus itself had been here. I felt stupid for everything I had believed before, and with that thought, I was ready to leave. I pushed back from the table to stand, when Hades firmly clamped his hand on my shoulder blade.

"The only way you'd be able to kill Zeus is if you kill Zerachiel…" he whispered.

"Zerachiel was hoping I would stall so he could kill him his self," I answered quickly, "and regardless, I'd become a fallen angel."

"You are smarter than Zerachiel gives you credit for!" he exclaimed, clapping his hands.

I glanced down at Enyo, who seemed to be hanging on by a thread. Pulling her to stand, I began to walk to the door when I felt the walls abrupt with a faint rumble. Zerachiel was descending because he knew I was here.

"You can't fly out of here without being noticed!" Hades yelled over the sound.

"You think I care?!" I yelled back.

I proliferated my wings, and scooped Enyo close to my chest. Developing to an aerial stance, I shot my left foot behind the right. As I crouched down, I took a deep breath. I had a generous amount between the floor and I, but my momentum collided with Zerachiel's. He fell to the purple lacquer floor, but growled as he shot up to chase after me.

Piloting through Hades Hall seemed to be quite tricky. I almost ran into several pillars and walls before finding an exit. I gushed out as fast as I could, with Enyo moaning in my arms. I could feel Zerachiel in pursuit of me, and I wondered why he hadn't attacked yet.

I spun into the air, and flew over the woods until I felt I was out of sight. Spotting Apollo's temple, I left Enyo at the steps near the entrance, then flew back into the air, making contact with Zerachiel.

The wind from the strength of his wings made it hard to stay in one place, so I flew above him, then spiraled down, with my hands out in front of me. I grabbed the middle of his back, and tried to crush where his wings were attached. With that failing me, I snatched him down near the ground, mustering as much strength as possible.

Zerachiel pressed his right hand against my face, then pushed my chin up as if he were trying to break my jaw. Grunting, I snapped out of his grasp and slammed him into the earth below. Without realizing how large of a crater we created, I let go of him and darted off, hoping to get the advantage.

Zerachiel spun to meet me, his eyes on fire with anger. I could see his pulse beating wildly in the veins on his neck. He hands were clinched so tightly that the knuckles shone white. He pierced his lips, and studied my demeanor.

"Why Zerachiel!?" I roared at him.

"Just because He's is God, doesn't mean…"

"Doesn't mean what?!" I roared again, "you are His creation!"

"I am my own man!" he roared back.

"If it weren't for Him, you wouldn't exist!" I pleaded.

"This is true, but I feel like I know what I'm doing since I've been doing it for a while."

"You won't get away with this!" I said, realizing how crazy he sounded.

"Who's going to stop me?" he said, mocking me.

"I'm sure He already knows!" I insisted.

"How much of a loss would it be to lose one crazy angel?" he sneered.

"An angel He spent time crafting together for one purpose," I answered him.

"I can be replaced!" he spat, grinning.

He laughed at himself, amused with my disappointment.

"Why have a set purpose, when you can rule?"

"You weren't created to rule, but to serve. That in it self is a pleasure of life," I retorted.

"I'm sure you get the most out of killing deities, you feel like you've done something great. But I am a messenger, and a messenger only…"

"He didn't craft you out of Himself to feel lesser than what you are. You're discontent with your purpose, Zerachiel. He gave you this job because He wanted to. It fit you. But obviously you don't see that."

"I see me ruling this place. And there isn't anything you can do about it…since you won't be completing your job. So there's a few things you can do. You can stay here, care free. You run back and tell "daddy." Or, I can kill you where you fly, which is probably the best thing to do."

I had completely forgotten what Hades had told me. I didn't think before flying off. But I figured the worst he could do was kill me. I spiraled up again, then made a straight shot to Zeus' temple. Landing, I showed no concern on how hard I came in.

Then I waited.

Surprised that Zerachiel wasn't flying right behind me, I looked up at Zeus who seemed to be staring off in the distance. As I climbed the stairs to his throne, I began to feel something was wrong.

Zerachiel was standing next to him, smirking, then he pushed Zeus off of his seat. The view from his face was normal, but there was a noticeable dark purple residue growing from the back of his head.

He had already been killed.

"You have a lot of explaining to do. Your relationship with this super human. Your lack of accordance for your job. And why you traveled realms without anyone's knowledge…" he said.

"You knew I was coming!" I roared, "Zerachiel, why are you doing this?!"

"I guess I'm a jealous prick?" he said, still smiling, "don't worry. You'll get your wish. You can be with her without worrying about breaking any rules."

Roaring as loud as I could, I charged towards him with as much intensity as possible. But the moment I reached him I flew throw the throne, and the temple. *Then I began to tumble to Earth.*

There was a burning sensation that started from my heart, then to my back up to the tips of my wings. And soon I could feel the heat from the atmosphere piercing my flesh. I grabbed at my throat, grasping for air as I seared downward.

I couldn't see where I was landing as I normally would have. Tears were streaming from my face, but they were lapped up as they evaporated once they hit the top of my cheek. My body felt limp, and now I was positive I was *falling*. I felt as if the layers of atmosphere had stripped the top of my skin off of my arms and face, and I was sure once I hit the ground, I was going to die.

With that thought, I closed eyes to think of Enyo. How much I loved her, even without knowing her well. Her smile, her voice, how soft she was. Her need to hold my hand. How she argued but looked into my eyes all at once.

The ground was nearing, and since I was sure this was my last day alive, I asked for forgiveness. I wasn't specific, I just asked. I couldn't believe everything that had taken place was out of my control now. And it seemed the only thing I regretted the most was not protecting Enyo. I smiled at the thought of her as gravity pushed me closer to the ground.

Nothing really is as it should be.

Chapter 7: Azrael, Fallen Archangel of Death

Each layer of atmosphere showered Azrael with condensation, I suppose from the speed he was falling. A cloud would form quickly, puffing out around where Azrael entered as he vertically seared through the air. The orange and golden rays of the sun brimmed on the edges of the last perforated clouds, adding to my angst. What a wondrous sight to behold, despite the conflict dealing with this event.

Azrael was falling steadily where Nathan guessed he would land. He seemed as if his body were limp, and he was twisting and flipping out of control as soon as he passed the troposphere. I looked to see if the people by this lake were watching, and noticed a small crowd forming. Some took pictures, while others began to call for first responders.

Soon sirens added to this chaos as Nathan eyed his friend's steady drop. I twisted the hem of my shirt once the small crowd developed more so. My nerves were strung out, and I wondered if Nathan could see this was driving me to tears.

Nathan grunted as he shot up into the air, his wings up heaving the sand around the lake a little. A few in the crowd sputtered in awe at this site. Hopefully he would catch him before anything else had been discovered.

Watching him retrieve Azrael in midair made me lose my breath. I was almost sure I was too late when I told Nathan what had happened. The impact from his catch caught him off guard, and both of them crashed into the lake we parked near, which Azrael could have drowned in. Nathan swam to the shore, with Azrael barely hanging on for life. Then Nathan sprawled out on his back, panting for air.

"He's still heavy," Nathan said in between breaths, "So he's fallen, but he still has his wings."

"I don't understand," I said, sitting next to Azrael and petting his face, "Zerachiel killed Zeus in our realm, how did…"

"Because He's God!" Nathan roared, sitting up, "You nim witted super beings are very forgetful, aren't you?"

Azrael was unconscious now. Nathan and I glanced at each other as the group of people came up to us, looking bewildered. I knew what he was thinking, so I placed my hand on his arm.

"Nothing to see," Nathan said, trying to explain.

"But…you…" a young man stuttered.

"Must've had your fair share of beer!" Nathan exclaimed, pointing at the young man's can., "and whatever else you do here…"

He looked at the can for a moment, then dropped it and ran off. Everyone else stood around and watched as we picked Azrael up and carried him to the cab. Nathan assembled himself in the front, then turned the key in the ignition. As we left, the E.M.T.'s arrived.

"Where are we going to go?" I asked, trying to keep my hair out of my face.

"We can't go back to his house, I have a feeling Zerachiel has either destroyed it or he will," Nathan answered.

He took a sharp turn onto the freeway, which caused a few cars to swerve. Then he rolled up all the windows. Nathan seemed as calm as ever, *even if he drove like a nut case.*

"This makes me wonder," I said, watching Azrael.

"Wonder what?" Nathan asked, peering in the review mirror at me.

"How long Zerachiel has been planning this…"

"Who knows, but now we need to figure out how to take him down. We have an advantage."

"What is that?" I asked, puzzled.

"Since Azrael didn't complete his job, and I'm sure other angels have been lied to, Zerachiel can't travel back here. One reason would be he wouldn't make it, he'd be shot down as soon as he left Olympus' atmosphere. The second reason is because he is of a higher ranking, if he isn't killed on sight, he would have to meet with God face to face. I don't believe he'd be able to handle that. So he'll stay where he is."

"What a coward…" I said in disgust.

Azrael moaned slightly as Nathan switched lanes to an exit. He curved the round about then went down the street. I wasn't sure where he was headed, but he was quiet and kept his eyes on the road.

Soon we were in a residential area. And then Nathan parked in front of a small but tidy house. He came to the right of the cab and opened the door. Then he pulled Azrael out, and put him on his shoulder. I followed behind him, trying to keep up. As soon we were in the front room, he carefully placed Azrael on a old rugged couch.

I sat down next to him instinctively, and ran my fingers through his curly hair. He opened his eyes in shock, but when he saw me he smiled and closed them again. I wondered if he knew he was dead or alive. Or even more so…if he meant to smile at me. I was just glad he was living, and wasn't seriously injured.

Azrael's pulse was racing wildly in his wrist, as he held a high temperature. His lips were slightly parted with his eyes slit. I started to examine his forehead and was shocked at my discovery. Not a single burn, scratch…abrasion. Nothing. He fell hundreds of thousands of miles from another realm, through atmospheric gasses…and he was spotless.

Azrael rolled over on the couch to lay on his stomach, then his left hand uncurled from the fist it once was in. I started to rub his back and study the structure of his muscles. I scooted up a little closer and placed both of my hands on him and started to rub it slowly.

Pushing his tattered shirt up, something caught my eye. Near the top-middle of his back it was extremely hot, but soft. Soft as if the skin were meant to be tender. I started to rub around this area, unsure of what would happen.

Maybe touching his back was a bad idea after all. Azrael shot up off of the couch, then fell on his knees screaming in pain. His wings seemed to have propagated and were flapping at a high speed.

This was causing everything in the room to be engulfed in what felt like hurricane strength winds. I tried to move closer to him to calm him down, but he stood up, grabbing his head, his vociferate ringing my ears. I was frightened at what I saw, but I couldn't help to gaze at Azrael in amazement.

Nathan came in, almost peeling the paint off of the wall to get a better grip. I noticed an older woman crouching under him, with her head to the floor.

When Nathan reached Azrael, he clamped his hands on his shoulders, and pressed him back down to his knees. Almost instantly, his wings corrugated into their original position. Azrael was panting for air as he gripped the carpet. You'd be a fool not to see the anguish he was in.

He stood up and swayed a little bit. Then he surveyed his surroundings. Nathan was still on his knees, shaking his head, and the older woman was now standing and gawking at Azrael in disbelief. Azrael looked down at me, but stumbled and tripped backwards over the table, his head hitting the edge of the couch.

He groaned at his insulted injury, then grabbed his head as he cursed. Heart strung, there I was by his side, helping him sit up. Azrael was still catching his breath, but found enough energy to embrace me. I felt secure, and comforted. And I could feel his strength emanating from his body.

"He is…." the old woman stuttered after a while, "He's…"

Nathan deeply sighed, then grabbed the woman by her hand to sit down.

"Azrael is the Archangel of Death," he said softly, "and he's recently fallen…"

"How could that be?" she said in a thick accent.

"Zerachiel…" I whispered, still stroking my fingers through Azrael's hair.

"Oh, Ya Ya, I'm sorry. I should introduce you two," Nathan said, gesturing towards me, "This is…"

"Whitney…" I said, eyeballing him, "pleasure to meet you."

"Pleasure," she said.

Nathan and I exchanged uneasy glances, but focused back on the conversation.

"Why has he fallen?" she asked.

"Zerachiel completed a job that was given to him. But he was tricked during the process," Nathan explained, "and now Zerachiel has killed her father, so he believes he can rule Olympus."

My sanity diminished when he mentioned my father, and I started to shake my head, even though it was too late.

"You…" Ya Ya said, pointing at me, "Are no ordinary woman."

She stood to walk to me, when she turned to look at Nathan in astonishment.

"And if you know them, what does that make you?"

"An Angel," Azrael said under his breath.

Nathan stood up quickly in defense, but sat back down with his eyes to the floor.

"You could have told me," Ya Ya said, sounding a little hurt, "What was I going to do?"

"No one can truly know who you are without getting in the way of your purpose," Azrael said, trying to sit up.

He paused, blinking frantically, then grabbed his right side in pain.

"I knew what you were seeking was more than just a project. You could have told me. I thought it was just…."

"We didn't want to upset you," Azrael said, speaking through his pain, "My job requires confidentiality."

Ya Ya seemed like she was having a hard time taking everything in at once. She slumped down then darted her eyes at me.

"You are Enyo," she said softly.

"I am."

"What now that your father is gone?" she asked me.

"I'm not sure…"

"Who would succeed him?" Nathan asked.

"Apollo or Athena," I answered.

"So that's who Zerachiel will try to kill next," Azrael added.

"It would probably be Athena first. She refuses to live on earth," I said.

"Well, that doesn't mean he can't get to Apollo, Hades had Manai following Azrael," Nathan pointed out.

"So lets go to the super market first," I said standing up.

Everyone shook their head at me.

"What about my brother?" I asked out of anger.

"You aren't supposed to be here," Azrael said standing to face me, "You're going out of your way to help something that should have been destroyed thousands of years ago."

"So after all you've told me, I shouldn't even be alive?!" I screamed at him.

I could feel hot tears pouring out over my lids and onto my face. Azrael grabbed me, and held onto me, but that only made it worse. I started to sob into his chest like a child who lost their favorite toy. All of these centuries, believing I was gift, when I was a hidden and forbidden cause.

"All those awful things I said to you…" I whispered, my tears abating, "You're right Azrael. I'm better off human!"

"There is one thing you can do to become mortal," Ya Ya said, pulling me from Azrael.

"What is that?" I asked, curious to know.

"You can go to the underworld, and sacrifice your immortality. Or perhaps take krythm, a painful but quicker process," she continued, walking into her kitchen.

She pulled out a stool and motioned for me to sit. Then she rummaged in her fridge and brought out a jar of huge maroon olives. I licked my lips and tried to concentrate on the conversation. But before I knew it, she had set a handful out on a napkin, and pushed it towards me. I reached down to devour one, when Azrael's hand came sweeping in front of me, grabbing half of my handful. I ignored his boy-like tendency, and focused back on Ya Ya.

"I could die doing this," I said, pressing the pit out of my olive.

"You'll be fine. But I recommend you get all of your siblings to do so, they'd benefit from it," she said, sucking on an olive as well.

"We'd all be killed the moment we set foot back into Olympus," Nathan said, stealing the remaining half of my olives.

I frowned at him, but smiled as Ya Ya set another handful of olives in front of me. Both Nathan and Azrael instinctively went to grab for them, but Ya Ya smacked their hands away.

"There's ways to defeat the underworld, especially if it is for the good of man…." Ya Ya said, now pouring glasses of juice for us.

"This isn't the hokie pokie, Ya Ya," Nathan said, looking serious.

"Nothing of the sort…." I mumbled, watching Azrael sneak another olive from my napkin, "Are you that hungry?"

He smiled as if he were a little kid. I had never seen him smile ear to ear like that.

Blushing, I allowed him to take another olive as he kissed me on my forehead. Ya Ya was watching us, but she was pleased with what she saw. She sat a huge glass of juice in front of him, then scooted mine to me. Then she whisked back around to the fridge, rummaging for other things to eat.

"What you'll need to be is strategic," she continued, pulling out a large package of roast beef, "witty, quick, and subtle. You can't go barging in since Zerachiel knows you might be coming back to attempt to defeat him."

"We said that already…Ya Ya…" Nathan said, frowning.

"Speaking of which, how is that even possible.,." Azrael asked.

"You need to mix what you would use to kill a god, with something that is highly effective on humans," she retorted, spreading mustard on a slice of bread.

"Bella Donna is the most potent poison known to man. There's literally no antidote. And it's extremely effective. Mixing that with krythm would probably do it," Nathan said, grabbing the first freshly made sandwich.

Azrael eyeballed him, then glared a little. I giggled at his reaction, and handed him my sandwich.

"The only issue is if it is too much or too little, the effects will counter act each other, and it would be pointless," I said, waiting for another sandwich.

"We could make…something like a bomb…." Nathan retorted.

"That would destroy everything in Olympus. It doesn't have a ground like Earth does…" I said, "Which isn't a bad idea…"

"But how?" Azrael said.

Everyone fell silent and looked at me. I blushed for a moment, then cleared my throat.

"I need time to plot that out…"

"We don't have time," Azrael answered, "we need something crazy-good….right now."

"He could be the bomb," Nathan said, unsure of our reaction.

Ya Ya clapped her hands together, and set a huge pile of sandwiches on a plate. I grabbed two, knowing that the rest would most likely go to the men.

"That's the only way," I said to myself, "we have to figure that out."

"Well Zerachiel doesn't like to settle. I'm sure by now he's slept with a few of the goddesses there. Perhaps you might catch his special attention," Nathan mentioned

I dry gagged at the thought, but neared my sandwiches closer when I saw Azrael and Nathan's reaction.

"You have to. And you don't have to sleep with him, but you have to pretend you want to…" Nathan continued.

"Wouldn't he figure that out…" Azrael said, displeased with the plan.

"Only if he resided in heaven, near God. He has cast himself out. So no, he wouldn't suspect a thing. Besides. He thinks all gods and goddesses are garbage. It's actually simpler than anything else we would have come up with. He'll automatically assume she's come to give homage…and tick tick…boom," Nathan said, with mustard all over his chin.

Ya Ya took a napkin, and gently rubbed it off. Then she kissed his cheek as she excused herself for a moment. I looked up at Azrael who was busy eating the remaining corner of his sandwich. He smiled at me, then looked at me as well with questioning eyes.

Nathan cheesed for a moment, then patted Azrael on the back before following after his mother.

"You were the last thing I thought about because I thought I was going to die. Which reminds me. How did you get to Nathan so fast?" he asked.

"He was on his way to you when he saw you and Zerachiel arguing above me. He landed after you left to Zeus' temple. And when he heard everything, he immediately went back to earth. The hardest part was guessing where you would land and fortunately for us, it wasn't far…."

"I owe him my life," Azrael said quietly.

I could see now why Azrael was so disciplined. He was committed to doing the right thing, no matter what. So then I wondered if I ever got in his way.

"Am I the biggest distraction…ever?" I asked sweetly.

"You are," he said, smiling at me and reading my thoughts, "I fought with the better of myself, but it isn't your fault I didn't realize Zerachiel was up to something. In fact I'm sure he hoped I would have killed you, or slept with you. Either way I would have become a fallen angel."

"Did it hurt?" I asked out of curiosity.

"I think outside of the physical pain I experienced, it hurt more to know I failed my Creator, I owe Him everything as well…"

"Maybe you fell for a reason," Ya Ya said, interrupting us, "Zerachiel will only expect you to fail now."

I blinked, as I thought she had left to give us some privacy.

"Two weapons out of three, one to go. What can I do?" Nathan said, walking in and frowning.

"What you do best," Azrael said standing up.

"That is…" Nathan said frowning.

Azrael shrugged as Ya Ya and I laughed a little.

I was glad they weren't concerned about what lay ahead. Sacrificing my immortality, and fighting a psychotic angel struck me as crazy. I was nervous about appearing in front of Zerachiel. Something in me made me feel he would pick up what was going on, and all of our efforts would be lost.

Enyo had only been to the Realm of the Forgotten once. And I guess I forgot how old Nathan was, Elmer treated him as if he were his younger brother. I smiled as they spoke with each other, obviously catching up. But I was anxious and slightly impatient with the task we had on hand.

"We need you to mix Bella Donna, with krythm…." Nathan said, handing him my small silver flask.

Elmer looked me right in the eye.

"If you would have killed her, you would have still been as you are," he said, taking the flask from Nathan, "and what a waste of beauty."

Enyo's eyes widened as she glanced at me. I shrugged, then followed Nathan and

Elmer into his shop. The god twisted within the shop moved, trembled the floor and pouring dust from all corners near the ceiling. Enyo excused herself and stood outside of the door to insure she wouldn't come into contact. There was probably more outside then there was in the shop.

"There's a way to keep her from getting sick or dying," Elmer said, adjusting his glasses, "half a dose of krythm would keep her guarded for life."

"Wouldn't that kill her?" both Nathan and I asked.

"It would kill her immortality... Unless you want to waste your time getting The Book of the Lost."

Nathan and I exchanged disgruntled looks, then turned to watch Elmer mix the two together.

"How long would it take?" I asked, nearing his desk.

The god moved again, rumbling the shop once more. I could hear Enyo cursing, and I watched her move out of the way near the edge of the realm. I excused myself, and went outside to fetch her.

She was looking down on earth with her arms crossed and I could tell she wasn't feeling the best.

"There's a simpler way to become mortal," I said, wrapping her cold body into a hug.

"How?"

"Half a dose of krythm," I whispered in her ear.

We were quiet while staring down, watching the clouds on Earth drawl by. Enyo smiled a little, but as usual I could hear everything going on below. After a while, Nathan came to retrieve the both of us. He looked concerned, so with haste we followed him back to Elmer's shop.

"I've mixed the two together, it should work. But I still think she should take half a dose of krythm…"

"What if it kills me?" she asked, looking bewildered.

"There's always a sacrifice in doing right," he said, cutting the pearl shaped pill in half, "but the process is painful."

I watched Enyo fight with herself. But then she nodded and smiled at Elmer.

"We're going to go to the back of the shop. Back there it's filtered, so there's no contaminates. At any rate, you have to be strapped down…"

"What is this…like…goddess intervention?" Nathan said, speaking out of concern, "How long will this take, we're short on time…"

"Five minutes," Elmer said, holding his hands up.

I looked to Nathan and gestured my inquisition. He nodded, noting he agreed.

We followed Elmer to the back of his shop. He flicked on a few switches, and a loud generator could be heard. It seemed this room was made out of glass or something like it. You could see in the distance the lake in which a lot of the spirits from here spawned, and you could see the face of the god I had been seeing for thousands of years.

Enyo seemed to be taken aback, as she was clinging onto my right arm. I pried her off, then guided her to the table where she would lay. Everyone was quiet, but more so because the dying god's eyes were wide open.

They weren't moving, or staring at us, but they were open looking up at something. Nathan peered in the direction it was looking and shrugged at me. Elmer walked over to retrieve a syringe for the krythm, then he flapped the goggles on his head. Next he asked Enyo to lay down, then he began to strap her in.

"Whatever happens Azrael," she said almost inaudibly, "I will always love you."

"I love you too, Enyo."

The shop shook again as this dying god moved his head to the side.

And now, I was nervous. I could see Enyo was trembling as she was crying. Then she began moaning uncontrollably out of fear once Elmer turned around to dispense the pill into a cup. He poured some form of a liquid into it, then stirred it together. Then he filled the syringe with the substance. As he turned, I could see how rigid she became. She took a deep breath and closed her eyes and started mumbling.

"You have to be completely still," he said, looking at her, "it will hurt like who knows what, but you're doing what's right."

She nodded, then looked over at Nathan and I with teary eyes. Nathan did a thumbs up and smiled, but I hit him in the back of his head. He knitted his brows together and shrugged.

"That's not a good form of support," I hissed at him.

"Neither is watching her!" he hissed back.

Elmer motioned for us to be quiet, then he injected the mixture to the left side of her neck. For a moment it seemed like nothing was going to happen, but her familiar glow I was used to started to fade. Nothing had ever scared me in my life, until I saw how much pain Enyo was in.

She shrieked like a spirit gone astray from where it rested. Her hips reared up violently as she fought the straps she was secured in. Then she began panting for air. Soon her eyes rolled in the back of her head, and that's when I jumped forward to the table.

"NO!" I roared, skimming my hands over her limp body, unsure that if I touched her something worse would happen, "You said…"

"She's fine…" Elmer insisted, pulling off his gloves, "She'll come to."

I ran one hand through my hair, then wiped the other hand down my face. Her natural complexion faded as she slowly started to turn that familiar purple. Her mouth parted open, almost as if it released her last breath.

A climatic tear oozed from her left eye, and slithered slowly down her lifeless cheek. Nathan attempted to pull me, but I pushed him off and reached out for her hand. My own began to shake as I gathered the horror of the moment.

But Nathan struggled to pulled me back from her then into the front of the shop. A disappointed Elmer stood behind his desk with both of his hands pressed on the clutter of papers that usually took up most of the space.

"It's worked before," he muttered in disappointment.

"With who?!" Nathan asked angrily.

"I've lost the only woman I ever loved…" I said in defeat.

"Give it some time," Elmer said impatiently.

"We need her!" Nathan screamed.

"More than you know," I said, trying to catch my breath.

It had been a few days since I had lost Enyo. Elmer figured since we stuck around, it was in his best interest to help clean up his shop. He kept explaining that after I killed Zerachiel, he would be out of a job, since he was the Messenger Angel intended for my purpose.

After cleaning, every evening I would sit next to Enyo and study her face, and body. Then I would hold her cold, lifeless hand in my own.

Today I cupped her dark purple face in my hands, pressing my forehead to hers. Then I kissed the bridge of her nose, down to her chin. I sat up, puling my fingers through her hair. Then my hands traveled to their usual spot. Her hand felt a little warm today, but it's possible I'm imagining things.

"I should have stopped you," I said close to her ear, "what was I thinking? I don't even believe…"

I stopped when I heard shuffling, but when I didn't see anything, I continued.

"I would give anything to have you back. To hold you again. To hear your voice…even if you were mad, and I know other men have loved you, but nothing like I do…." I said chuckling.

I wiped my face and looked up again, hoping I wasn't being watched.

"I love you Enyo," I whispered, noticing the lingering voices traveling closer, "So much…"

Nathan stood at the door way with a concerned look about his face. He smiled, but I'm sure he had an idea of what I was doing. I wiped my shameless tears and walked into the shop with Nathan. We still had so much to do.

The fourth day, Nathan and I decided it was best to leave. We were going to have to take Zerachiel down by ourselves. Before we departed, I kissed Enyo's forehead and rubbed my hands through her hair. Then I pressed my head to hers, trying not to cry. I could hear Nathan walk up behind me. So I sat up, and flattened out her hair again.

"I thought…."

"Maybe it's what she wanted…" he said quietly.

"Maybe…"

Even in death she was beautiful. I wish there was more I could have done, and I also felt as though I wouldn't be able to go on with out her. So I followed Nathan into the front of the shop and began to pack my bag. Looking outside, I noticed Elmer standing on the edge where the gatekeeper used to stand. He was looking around the rim of his realm, almost as if he were taking everything in one last time.

Soon the storms in the distance made their way in our location. It was really nothing but hard rain, and it was enough to change anyone's mood. I sat down on the floor of the shop; it felt like packing was taking forever. Nathan had joined Elmer outside, and motioned for me to come. As soon as I stood up, I heard a noise in the back, but I ignored it.

The breeze and the rain on the cliff seemed to make me emotional as well. Even when I thought I would die, I couldn't stop thinking about Enyo. And all the effort I put into sparing her life was for nothing.

I looked back at the shop, then became hysterical when I saw Enyo slowly walking towards me. With that, she started to run to me. As soon as she was close, she buried her head into my chest and wrapped her arms around my back. I hugged her like I would never see her again, and I pressed my cheek into her ear.

"It would have been nice if someone had been there to take those straps off, but I figured it out…" she said backing up to rub her wrist, "I feel old…"

"How did you…?" I asked, scanning her face for answers.

"I just needed time, I guess," she answered shyly, "But I'm glad you waited for me."

I sputtered out in laughter and tears, and hugged her tightly again. We all honestly thought she was *dead*. And Elmer was smiling, which was rare. I felt as if I'd be forced to covet her the remainder of my days, and now I am finally able to *love her*. Once we let go she looked up at me, then at Nathan and Elmer.

"I'm ready," she said.

Zerachiel had no idea we were on our way. Elmer insisted he couldn't know because as we had discussed before; he was too chicken to leave Olympus knowing that his life was in peril.

"Is there anything else we need?" Nathan asked while we were standing on the edge of the realm.

"Faith," Elmer said, smiling at all of us, "Azrael is fallen for a reason."

I again, frowned at Elmer. It was classic for him to say something under-motivating in pure admonishment. We all nodded, and prepared to descend, when Elmer caught me by my shoulder.

"It takes about 5 minutes for that elixir to actually work. And since it is technically a bomb, you have five minutes to leave Olympus, otherwise you will all die with him," he said with concern.

Then he smiled and stepped back to wave.

Nathan looked at me with his brows knitted again and his mouth open, and Enyo looked defeated as well.

"Why is everyone frowning at me," I said in frustration.

Nathan shook his head, and leapt into the air while spiraling down towards Olympus. I scooped Enyo up under my arm and followed suit. This time we were taking it slow. If we flew into Olympus too fast, everything would begin to shake. Then, Zerachiel would either be warned or be waiting for us. Nathan motioned to a canopy for a safe landing. I followed him into the woods, and since it was dark, we figured we were harder to spot.

At least for a moment.

"I'm exhausted," Enyo complained once we landed, "I'm not used to this."

"Here," Nathan said, tossing her a large brown flask, "Drink up."

She eyeballed it, then scrunched her nose up.

"Just drink it," I whispered to her.

She nodded, then gagged and spit it out.

"What is this?" she asked, attempting to wipe the taste from her tongue.

"Pegasus saliva. Provides natural energy, even for humans," Nathan answered, cheesing, "I'm kidding…it's red bull…"

I laughed at her reaction as she took a few sips. Then she handed it to me, and sat on the ground in the moss.

"It doesn't give you wings…I was hoping for two more…" Nathan said, "So, what's the plan?"

"I can't summon a chariot, Azrael needs to drop me off as close as possible…"

she said, rubbing her hands on her knees.

"And then what…." I asked, remembering the plan.

"I have to pretend I want him…." She said, glaring up at me, "I don't find him attractive."

I believed what she said, but I didn't like that she had to be so close to him.

"Zerachiel's into himself right now," Nathan explained, "she'll be the least of his worries."

Enyo stood up and dusted herself off. Then she stretched, and smacked me in the head.

"Let's go" she said, taking a stance.

"I'm going to find someone that can help us. You need to stay around the temple until she's done the deed. Zerachiel's going to come rearing out of there like an angry hornet once he finds out what she's done," Nathan said, picking up his belongings, "And I'm positive he has help."

"What will your signal be?" I asked, turning to Enyo.

"Here," Nathan said, handing her a golden rod, "it's a flare."

"From Saturday Night Fever?" I asked, frowning at it.

"From Ya Ya," he smiled, shoving one in my hand as well, "It's got small amounts of krythm in it as well."

I raised an eyebrow as Nathan walked off, waving.

"Five minutes!" I called after him.

The idea would work well since all of the temples had an area in which there wasn't a roof. I looked to Enyo, who seemed unsettled, and impatient.

"Do you think we'll be successful?" she asked, looming closer to my face.

I scooped up the back of her head and kissed her. Finally, nothing else really seemed to matter except us. Soon Enyo's hands were up my shirt, then on my chest. And she slowly dragged her nails down to my pants. I pushed back gently to break the kiss, then smiled at her uncontrollably.

"Let's leave it at that," I said softly, "We have work to do."

I pressed her body into mine to ascend into flight, and soon we were soaring over the country side. Then I landed near another wooded area by her father's temple. Enyo pulled off her bag, and changed into a sheer gold and white chiton. She then tossed her hair around and shoved her bag into my arms.

"I hope this isn't an all night affair…." I said, trying to grab after her hand.

"I hope he doesn't touch me, I'm not sure how I'll react…" she answered quietly.

"You won't have to bare anything you normally wouldn't have to."

At least I hoped.

Chapter Eight: The Book of The Lost

I could see enough from my view in this tree, but I felt like I was being watched. The branches near me had been rustling for about twenty minutes. Then finally, a bright orange bird appeared then flew off. *Nervous for nothing.*

I looked over at Zeus' temple, then to Aphrodite's as I watched her walk out of the entrance and scan the thickly branched forest. My hope was that she wouldn't see me sitting up so high, but the only light she had to view me came from the moon. It seemed so close, closer than it usually is on earth. It was almost as if I could touch it.

My worst fear at the moment was happening. I saw her peer into the branches, then head into the forest. After about 20 minutes she made it to our camp out, cursing about the leaves and scrapes she gathered along the way. As I suspected she would do, she stopped at the tree I was sitting in and looked up.

"I know why you're here, Azrael," she cooed softly, "it's best you listen to what I have to say."

"Yes ma'am," I said jumping down to meet her.

Aphrodite stood back for a moment to examine me, then she smiled and moved closer. I flinched as she traced her thin fingers up my chest to my chin, then she ran them slowly across my lips. Catching her hand, and shoving it to her side, I frowned at her.

"Fine..."she said sounding defeated, "But Zerachiel may know you're here. Earlier he sent out a militia of centaurs to keep watch through the night. It's best you either hide in my chambers, or leave this realm."

"I'd rather die if those are my choices, especially the first," I scoffed at her.

She knitted her nicely trimmed eyebrows together then bit her lip.

"I know what you've heard of me, and although this may be true, we are on the brink of annihilation. Sleeping with you is the last thing on my mind, no matter how attractive you are..." she said, almost as if she forced herself to do so.

"I have enough krythm with me to do you in if you don't keep your word. Now, is there a roofless area in your chambers that allows me to see...?"

It was obvious that male dominance rendered an attraction in a goddess; Enyo always seemed intrigued when I was clearly being serious. I saw a playful light dance in Aphrodite's eyes, which disgusted me even more. So I remained quiet as she continued studying me up and down. Then she tipped her head ruefully to the side to answer.

"Clear onto the next temple, which is Zeus'," she answered, "And I give you my word, if I don't do as I've promised you can take my life."

I nodded at her as I gathered up the rest of my belongings. Then I slowly followed her into her temple and all the way to her chambers. The décor seemed to be nothing but pillars of sheer pink and purple curtains that were blowing softly in the night breeze. I looked perplexed as she smiled to pass me. Then Aphrodite walked to her bed and pulled the sheet over while prompting me to sit.

"No one comes back here unless..." she said, gesturing to the bed.

I stood up as quickly as possible and felt the back of my pants. She grinned at me in amusement, then pushed me to sit back down.

"You'll be fine, I'm sure you've dealt with worse."

"And where will you be?" I asked, trying to ignore that the bed may be moist.

"An ear away. You'll be able to warn me, and I'll be able to do the same," she said, "I'm sure my sister will be fine. She is the goddess of war."

"Shouldn't it trouble you that a power crazed angel is attempting to take over Olympus?"

It was easy to since Aphrodite wasn't used to having serious conversations. She shook her head at me as if I were teasing then disregarded my inquiry as she left.

So I sat on her bed in silence. From time to time she would walk by with a group of giggling women, but none of them paid me any mind. After a while I turned to get a better view of Zeus' temple, when I heard a deep voice at the entrance of Aphrodite's temple. I panicked slightly as I stood up from her bed. I wasn't sure if I'd be able to defend myself..

Aphrodite was talking loud enough for me to hear, but I remained fearful, remembering my chances of beating a centaur were very slim. So I started to back further into her chamber until I was near the garden in the back. As soon as my heel hit the dirt, both the centaur and Aphrodite fell silent. I cursed at myself, then rummaged in my bag for the golden flare.

By the time I found it, I heard hooves coming closer. My pulse thumped wildly, causing me to perspire. How fortunate that I was graceful at this time. I fell back and rolled into the middle of the garden, with the golden flare out of my reach. I made myself skeptical of my own moves, realizing my next may be my last. Their shuffling feet came closer as I tucked myself behind a bush.

Aphrodite came behind the centaur looking for me in confusion. I realized out of my fear, I didn't hear a thing she was saying. So when she called for me I did not answer.

"Tell him we're prepared to help him in any way we can. We also have a large quantity of those golden flares Nathan is so accustomed to."

"Wait!" I said jumping up, unaware of my appearance, "I wasn't sure if you were after me…so I hid."

"You could have flown away," the centaur said, walking towards me.

As it came closer, I began to realize…it was a female. She smiled once she reached me, then she helped dust off the leaves and petals I had collected while running.

"Just because I can fly, doesn't mean I should," I retorted.

Aphrodite walked closer to us with a concerned look on her face.

"Whatever effort you all put forth to insure Enyo wouldn't come into sexual contact may not be averted. Zerachiel has a way with words. I'm hearing from others that he's instituted any female he comes into contact with must bear him a child as well. He refuses to spill his seed."

My eyes traveled to her belly, then to her eyes. She glared, and shook her head quickly so Sheila wouldn't notice. Pretending I hadn't seen anything, I focused back into the conversation.

"Enyo isn't of any concern to him. And she wouldn't allow that to happen," I said, a little high strung and hopeful.

"Zerachiel's a bewitching character, I assure you," the centaur spoke up, "and perhaps a proper introduction is needed. My name is Sheila."

I nodded, my thoughts still on Enyo. No need in explaining my silence, so I turned my attention back to Aphrodite.

"You're not there, Azrael…" Aphrodite shot out, "you can hope all you want…"

"I'm sure if something was wrong, I would know by now," I said in confidence.

Aphrodite and Sheila exchanged glances, then Sheila smiled at me.

"He has…some what of a spell on Zeus' temple. The only thing that can be seen from there is the flare, which is why Nathan gave it to you and to her," Sheila spat.

"So you've already talked with Nathan then? And has anyone located Zerachiel through all of this?" I asked, obviously confused.

"Yes. Tonight, and then prior to your return. We've been watching Zerachiel fly back and forth from here and heaven. So we became suspicious. But we never expected anything like this…" she continued.

"I see…" I said solemnly.

The three of us fell quiet, then Aphrodite prompted me to follow Sheila to their compound, a place she suggested was safer than here. As I walked down the steps to her temple, I noticed a handful of centaurs standing near her front gardens. I smiled and nodded, unsure of what to say. And following them seemed to take *forever*. I wish I could ascend into the air, and fly overhead, but I had a feeling Zerachiel would see, hear, or feel me.

Once we arrived at their camp, I began to follow Sheila into her tent. Once we entered, Nathan stood up smiling, then offered me a seat. I again was lost.

"I had to find them and make sure we were on the same level. Since I kept hearing rumors that there was a centaur militia," Nathan said, clapping his hands on my shoulders.

shook me as I slowly began to smile. I never knew what was going on.

"There is," Sheila said, parting between us, "they're all male centaurs."

Nathan shrugged then sat back in his previous position.

"We're not here to fight," I said, remembering Enyo, "we're here to destroy Zerachiel."

"You can still see Zeus' temple from here, but it's better if you're further away. Zerachiel's centaurs have a tendency to check Aphrodite's temple along their route of inspection. It was unwise of her to bring you there," Sheila retorted, "she may have done that to save her own life; she's more than likely pregnant by him."

"HA!" Nathan said, standing up to retrieve a golden flare.

"She was offered a position as his "Wife" as she put it."

I shook my head at that thought, then finally sat down.

"So what about Enyo?" I asked, looking at Nathan then Sheila.

"I think she'll be ok…"

Sheila rushed out of the tent without another word. Seconds after she exited, the screams of the other centaurs in the camp began to fill our ears, until the sound became unbearable. I ran outside only to run into a large, male centaur. He glared at me with the greatest intensity, and lunged forward to charge at me. I instantaneously flew up into the air with all my might.

As I flew overhead I was caught off guard by a spear. Maneuvering away took a lot of strength, and I flew into a tree. I could see Nathan aviating with ease while dodging several spears. He caught one that passed him on his left side, and darted it back, then came to help me. Nathan broke a few branches then flew off again to help fight.

Once I was free, I flew above the canopy of the woods, then spiraled down, tackling another male centaur as I landed on the ground. I noticed a few of the females had been killed, and Sheila was on her side, injured, but still firing off arrows. I ran up to her to push her right side up, but she pulled me down onto my knees and looked me in my eyes.

"My back legs are broken," she said sadly, "and I will most likely die, but go into my tent. There's a wooden lever that allows the ground beneath to open into a passage. Right at the entrance are to large sacks full of golden flares. Take those, and follow the tunnel until you reach Zeus' garden. Unless someone follows you, you'll be hidden out of sight."

She motioned for me to go, and as soon as I was a few feet away, a male centaur rammed into her, killing Sheila on contact. I pulled Nathan's hand and dragged him into the tent, then located the lever. As soon as I pulled it, I spotted the bags filled with golden flares, and handed a sac to Nathan. I kicked at the inner lever, which closed the door, then I tugged Nathan as I began to follow the tunnel as I was instructed.

"I have to go back!" Nathan screamed at me, ripping his self free from my grasp.

"So you can die? I need you!" I roared back at him.

Nathan stop, showing he was contemplative. Instead of turning back, he shook his head and continued to follow the tunnel.

"What were we going to do anyway," he scoffed, "male centaurs murder angels just for the fun of it. They would have killed us both."

I was silent whenever Nathan was ranting. Adding to his frustration only made him angrier. Soon I could see how close we were to the back entrance of Zeus' garden. I stopped and peered out to see if anyone was on guard. Then I sat the flares down, and rested against the carved rock. I examine my friend and noticed Nathan's lip had been busted at the bottom. Not only that, he had a huge gash above his left eye. But I was positive he wasn't as tired as I was.

"How long do we have to wait?" Nathan asked, breaking the silence.

"Until she lights the flare," I answered.

As soon as it left his lips, a golden flare shot up into the air over Zeus' temple. I stared up in wonder as it twirled upwards, glittering as it faded. Nathan picked up his sac to walk out when I stopped him

"He knows," I said, heavily disappointed.

We both peered up at the temple, still seeing no one was outside. Nathan glanced over at me, then cursed. He wanted us to come, and my main concern more than ever, was the safety of Enyo.

Both Nathan and I were in complete disbelief. More so because the confinement was completely empty, except for the main hall down at the end. Every single chamber we passed was bare, and as we neared the end I began to feel weak for what we would find.

Nathan pushed the door open first, and in defense flew up into the air, evasive of the lightening blasts in his direction. I pulled the cord to the flare in my hand, but Zerachiel used the scepter he held to knock it out. I followed Nathan's lead by flying into the air as a defense, but I was having difficulty avoiding be struck by lightening.

Nathan shot up as high as he could, then began to spiral down to Zerachiel, dodging near misses when he was struck in his left wing. He tumbled onto the marble floor, and skid outside to the stairs near the garden. Then Zerachiel turned his attention to me.

"You thought I wouldn't figure out your little scheme?" he said, firing random shots in my direction.

I maneuvered around them, but the last one caught my foot. I collided with a pillar and came crashing down onto the floor.

"You can't get away with what you're doing, Zerachiel!" I screamed at him.

He took a step, then shot another lightening bolt at me. I rolled out of the way, and stood up with my back pressed against the pillar I just hit.

"I can, and I will!" he roared at me.

He took the scepter and pointed at my neck. I could see the anger rising in his eyes, and he began to smile.

"I'm sure if you pray, you'll be back where you came from!" he said, cackling.

At that moment, I could have hoped to die. But what he wasn't expecting was Nathan *and* Apollo coming behind him. Apollo quickly unsheathed his sword and knocked the scepter out of his hands.

Instinctively, Zerachiel ascended into the air to his better advantage. Nathan flew up to meet him, but as soon as he got close, Zerachiel kicked him in his head. I watched in agony as Nathan's body went limp and fell to the ground below. I shot up from where I lay to catch him, and had been almost too late.

Laying him on the dirt of the garden, I fixed my gaze on Zerachiel when I noticed Enyo tied to a tree.

As I began to fly over to her, I could feel the rushing of Zerachiel's wind from his pursuit of me. Her hand was out just enough that I was able to catch the vile she had been holding onto. With all my strength, I forced myself up into the tree, then free into the air until I was sure Zerachiel was behind me.

Apollo stood underneath us, and threw a spear at Zerachiel. Like a tooth pick, it snapped on impact. Then Zerachiel took the tip of it and threw it back to Apollo, who dodged it. With the sharpened edge, Apollo ran to cut Enyo loose, when Zerachiel decided to go after him.

"Remember who you're after!" I roared after him.

He stopped for a moment, and looked up at me.

"I know what you're going to do!" he screamed at me, "you will not stop me!"

I began to think to myself…since he obviously knew what we were doing, would it hurt to try something else? I wanted to end this without dragging it on anymore, so without another word, I began to fly to the underworld. As I expected, he was right behind me, literally flying over me. I shot down to the entrance and as I entered, I slammed into a wall. I scurried to stand up and began to run down the corridor to Hades' hall.

As I entered the room, I found Manai hovering over what appeared to be an unconscious Hades. Shocked at my discovery, I ran up to him and took him by his shoulders.

"Where is The Book of the Lost!" I yelled.

"Underneath this table. But only the pure of heart can read from it, and use it's powers if its life is in peril. Are you in danger!?" he yelled back, looking bewildered

The walls of the room began to shake uncontrollably, then started to tear away as Zerachiel entered the chamber we were in. Manai nodded at me, and tapped on the table. It flipped over, exposing the hiding place of the book. Without a second thought, I jumped on to grab it, but Zerachiel was right there.

I pressed my hand onto his head to push him away, but he punched me in my shoulder blade and grabbed for the book. I positioned myself to kick him in the face. Then I opened it up to the first page and looked at Manai.

"The inscription reads, that if your life is in peril, you can trap him in the bottom of the table for a fragment in time!" Manai screamed.

Zerachiel and I scuffled once more as he clawed to reach this book. I panicked and kicked him in his shoulder, then looked at Manai.

"How long!" I yelled, kicking Zerachiel in the face again.

"JUST DO AS I SAY!" Manai roared, "speak his name, his crime, and it should work!"

"Zerachiel, messenger angel of heaven, is trying to kill me, and rule Olympus!"

Zerachiel growled at the top of his lungs and hurled his self at me once more. As soon as he hit the middle of the table, the legs flipped from the bottom began to mold themselves around him. Strange to see the table levitating as it swallowed this angry angel.

As the table shook and groaned, Zerachiel reach for my leg. But I kicked and freed myself from his grasp. Manai snatched me off of the table before it switched over, trapping Zerachiel beneath it. It shook violently for a moment as Zerachiel growled out in anger. Then his wings began to spread across the top until they were still, like stone.

I took a deep breath, trying to take in everything that I saw, then I glanced down at the book and Manai.

"What the hell!" I roared at him, "If I were Hades, I wouldn't want anyone to find this either!"

"Don't get too excited. It's only temporary. You have to leave Olympus, now," Manai said, dragging Hades' body out of the disheveled room.

"Wait…What? He's trapped there, forever, right?" I asked, helping him.

"No…only for four days," Manai explained, pulling Hades' body onto a boat, "You have bigger fish to fry."

"What do you mean?" I asked, following behind him onto the boat.

He pushed me off, then closed the gate.

"The other first descedants, of those fallen angels? The" titans" as we like to call them? He's freed them," Manai said, looking for a paddle.

"Fuck!" I said out loud.

I grabbed my hair in frustration and pulled back a little. It was the last thing I wanted to hear.

"Don't worry, they're coming here. It's gonna be a huge family reunion. Then after they destroy, rape, pillage, and kill everything here only THEN will they be going to Earth."

"What happened to Hades?" I said, pointing at him.

"That's what happens when you do when do bad business. Hades has always been a sucker for a good idea, but he always gets the blunt end of the stick when it's all said and done."

"Is he dead?" I asked.

"Close, but he'll recover…Azrael…I have to go, my friend. Be safe."

He pushed off the shore and waved. Everything seemed to never go the way I planned it. First Zerachiel turns against his own Creator, and heaven. Then he releases the

Titans. What else could possibly happen?

I flew back over to Zeus' temple to find Apollo and Enyo sitting next to each other. When I landed, I could see Nathan was recovering, but still hurt.

"Can you fly?" I asked, touching his back.

He slapped my hand off of him and backed up a little.

"Yes, I was just flying around. It hurts like shit, but I don't have a choice."

"Is he dead?" Apollo said looking around to the sky.

"He's trapped under Hades' table," I said, holding the book up, "for…"

"Four days," Apollo and Enyo said together.

"We're are so…totally…fucked!" Nathan said, kicking a bush.

"We can defeat him, and his relatives," I said, holding up the vile, "We need more of this."

"Ya, well, Elmer quit because he knew what was going to happen!" Nathan said, still sounding hysterical.

Apollo looked shocked at the announcement and stood to his feet.

"Who else can probably make more?" Apollo asked, showing his concern.

"Another soothsayer," Enyo chimed in.

"And where do we find one?" I asked with my hands on my hips.

"My Ya Ya."

Enyo smiled at his answer, but I became angered, and began to mentally judge what he had said.

"You're an angel, and found refuge with a witch?" I asked in frustration.

"What did you just say?" Nathan said.

Nathan had made his way into my face, and as I expected, we were having a stare down. I took a deep breath to speak when Apollo pushed his sword between the two of us, and firmly set his foot down. He looked at Nathan, then at me and shook his head.

"Now is not the time," he spoke softly, "whatever laws Nathan has broken has nothing to do with what we need."

"Sorry, Nathan," I mumbled.

"Ya…ok."

Nathan shot up into the air and out of sight. I sighed deeply, and motioned for Enyo to come with.

I grabbed Enyo, and shot up into the air, almost catching up with Nathan. Then he darted down as he made his landing known. Enyo closed her eyes and held her breath as I began to descend. As soon as I was close enough, I halted, which landed us floating in Ya Ya's living room. She was sitting on the couch smiling up at us sweetly.

Nathan sat down next to her and glared at me.

"I said I was sorry," I said, dusting myself off.

"I know, but…" he said, seeming somber, "I didn't have anyone until I found her. Then I found you. You don't know how much she means to me….but you're right. I disobeyed the laws of heaven, but she loves me. And I love her."

"I spoke out of turn from anger and disappointment…."

"We failed," Nathan said, sounding even sadder than before, "We've just jeopardized the world…"

"You have four days, and you need a large quantum of the mixture. That isn't a problem," Ya Ya said, interrupting Nathan, "It won't take me long to make it, you need to figure out how to distribute it."

Everyone grew quiet at the fact she knew what just happened. Attempting to ignore her comment we turned to each other again.

"We have six that we have to kill now. Six…" Enyo said, rubbing her arms, "If Zerachiel thinks we're coming back, I'm sure the others know as well."

"Why are there only five?" I asked, incontestably ignorant.

Ya Ya smiled again, and pulled The Book of the Lost out of my hands. She flipped through it briefly, then when she found what she was looking for, she handed it to me.

"It says the story is about the history of the titans," she said.

"The Titans?" I asked, a little irritated with it, "They're not the same as those fallen angels."

"Actually," Ya Ya said, still smiling, "They are descendants. All mythology is circulated around the truth. Though it may not be the same names, crimes, or culture, the "Titans" are those first descendants."

"Well he can't release them from hell," Nathan said, looking confused as well, "He doesn't have that kind of power."

"Remember," Enyo interrupted, "These are Titans. Your angels can only be released by your God. Our Titans can be released by the god who's on top of things in Olympus. So even though they have the same origin, *they're just descendants*. What Zerachiel is trying to do is rule under our realm as it's god without the consequences of trying to rule Earth. These Titans are the first descendants, along with Zeus. Zeus tricked them into destroying the world and Olympus, and had no other choice but to imprison them for life. He is the first of the six."

"He's not going to get away with it," I said, blinking at everything Enyo explained, "God won't allow it."

"He's allowing it for a reason," Ya Ya said calmly, "Great triumph is always followed by failure amassed in great devastation. He will rise, but he will be crushed by his own glory. Why go after him, when he'll fail by his self. Besides, I know for a fact God knew what he was going to do way before what he's doing now."

There wasn't much else to add to that. It was a true statement. I looked at Enyo and could see the wheels turning in her head. We had to destroy Zerachiel, and these Titans once and for all. In my honest opinion, it should have been done a long time ago.

Our next big issue was getting a hold of Hermes, and Io. It wasn't so much that we couldn't, we were concerned about their safety, on Olympus, and traveling to Earth. Since four days wasn't a long time, Enyo agreed to travel back to her apartment, and find her communication globe to contact Hermes.

In four days, what we came up with would decide the fate of Olympus and this world as well. I had no idea how Zerachiel would act once he was freed from that table, my only hope was that it gave us a bigger advantage than it seemed.

Chapter Nine: As Useless as Io

I hated waiting on people, especially when we had something important to do. Azrael flew me back to my tiny apartment, and to our surprise, everything was torn apart. Luckily, I found my globe, but I felt it was safer to contact Hermes at Ya Ya's house.

I was sitting on her porch, wrapped in a jacket that was obviously too big for me. Being mortal for two days seemed to be even more lack luster than living for thousands of years. It felt like I couldn't get enough sleep, and what was worse….*I couldn't think of anything in defeating Zerachiel.*

Shivering I realized it was beginning to snow. I would give anything to be somewhere else, but here. I saw Hermes fly up ahead and land on the tree across the street. Then, almost with caution, he flew towards the battered car garage on my left. As I looked down the street I could see Io slowly walking up, but acting wary to everything she saw.

One would think after the thousands of years Io lived, nothing would surprise her. She stopped to cross the street and backed up when a car came zooming past. I shook my head at how ridiculous she was being, so I stood and waved her down. Hermes had already changed back to human form and was standing by my side when Io finally made it to us.

"Enyo, Hermes…" she said quietly.

"Inside," I said, swinging the screen open.

We were all startled by the loud snoring emitting from Azrael's open mouth. I laughed and tossed a pillow on his face, but he did not budge. I figured the best place to talk to Io and Hermes would be in the kitchen, so I pulled out a few chairs around the table, then sat down. Io was looking around as if she were extremely displeased with everything she saw. Then she looked at me and smiled sweetly, which caught me off guard.

"It's so good to know you're alive," she said, reaching out to pat my hand.

I couldn't guard my apprehension, so instead of reacting how I wanted, I smiled and nodded.

"I didn't think anyone was left alive…" she started off, "when I discovered my husband was dead, I wasn't sure what to expect."

"You never came into contact with…" I said, trying to follow her story.

"Of course I did," she said in disgust, "I wish I hadn't."

I raised my eyebrow when she rubbed her belly. Then she flattened her clothes over her legs and looked at me.

"Everyone is dead. Except for Athena and Apollo. I'm sure you know, he lives here. And Athena went into hiding. We're just not sure where Hera is…oh…and…Aphrodite killed her self…." She continued.

"She said she refused to give her body to him," Hermes said out of nowhere, "of all times…"

"Let's not talk about what she normally would have done, Hermes," I said, nodding at him.

"Do you know of all your father has done?" Io said, staring at me with the up most intensity, "Did you know that Zerachiel helped him?"

"What!" Hermes and I said in unison.

"Zerachiel would convince Zeus to do something foolish in exchange for a woman he wanted. No matter how risky it was, Zeus *always* agreed. It's cost him his life. As you can imagine, Zeus was the first to die."

"Zerachiel wanted it hush-hush. So that if anyone asked, they wouldn't be able to find out," I said, agreeing with her.

"Well, he didn't pay me any mind. He believed in gods, and other deities, but not a human cursed with agelessness. He insisted I was crap, and I'm convinced he feels that way about all humans…" she said, rubbing her belly again.

I swear, if she rubs her belly one more time…

"So…did he mention anything about coming here?" I said, trying to keep the conversation between us.

"No. He said if he tried to come here, he'd die as soon as he left Olympus' atmosphere. He wants to reign there."

"He can't," Azrael said, cutting in, "Especially if he's killing everyone."

I looked up to a sleepy eyed angel. He was grimacing, but took time to smile at me.

"Well…" Io said, rubbing her belly again, "he did mention he planned on impregnating some of the nymphs. So not all of them are dead…"

I curled my lip up at this information, then looked up at Azrael who was grinning from ear to ear.

"What's funny about that?" I said, pushing him a little.

"He's really trying to make a name for his self," he explained, "if any of those babies survived, we'd be fighting a thousand year war."

"And that's funny because…?" I asked again.

"It isn't. It would be hell….can you imagine?" Io said, widening her eyes.

Quite the actress, she is.

"Is there anything you can tell us about the Titans?" Azrael asked, sitting across from me.

"There are my husband's brothers," Io answered.

"I thought Hades and Zeus were related," Hermes added, "That doesn't make any sense."

"Hades was spawn up from the fear of the people that worshipped Zeus. One of Zeus' sons had died, and since Zeus didn't have anyone else to push around, he sent a witch to The Realm of the Forgotten," Io said, sounding mystical, "Hades was more like…Zeus' bitch."

"Wait," I said, holding my chest as if I lost my breath, "Hades is nothing more than a spirit?"

"And all gods and goddesses are nothing but failed descendants of 6 fallen angels. They felt that life was purposeless, so temples were built on Olympus and on Earth. If you don't know the origin of your birth, I consider it nothing," Io added, "to succumb to reality after years of living a fantasy is hard."

Funny, I hadn't asked her that…

"So why were you cursed with agelessness?" I question, noticing she ignored my previous inquiry.

"I wouldn't give myself to Zeus *at first*. He had put a curse on me, hoping I would change my mind. I refused him again. But his efforts in attempting to care about Perseus made me reconsider. So I had a loveless, childless, anger filled marriage for thousands of years….," she said becoming teary eyed, "the only thing I could truly cling to was his fate if he ever died. Only then would I be free."

"Where was it said that gods don't die?" Azrael asked, grinning again, "You were all bastard children of fallen angels…"

"In the belief of a crafted reality," I answered him.

He nodded, then retreated to Ya Ya's fridge. Io rubbed her belly once more then caught me watching her. She bit her lip for a moment, then shook her head.

Irritated with her repeated action, I grabbed her hand and pulled it away from her stomach.

"Are you pregnant?" I asked, noticing she was showing.

"I think so…"

"Either you are or you aren't," Hermes said sternly, "who's the father?"

"I can't tell you," she said, trying to be vague.

"And why is that?" I hissed, showing that I was irritated.

"I don't know who's baby it is!" she shrieked, "Zerachiel…."

"You said you didn't sleep with him!" I said slamming my hands on the table.

"It's either Zeus' or Apollo's!" she said, backing up in defense, "I would never!"

I was pissed. With everything we were trying to do to stop the worst from happening, there was a possibility she might be pregnant. Even it was my father's offspring, our goal was to obliterate the entire race of what I could now consider fallen deities.

I shook my head at her, but tried to remain calm. I began to see why Azrael was so enamored to *hate* my race. We were a breed of fallen angels who didn't obey their Creator. And all we ever seemed to do was make a mess out of everything.

"It's hard to believe all of this," I said quietly, "growing up thinking we were on top, when we were all a huge mistake."

Hermes excused his self from the table, and I was positive he wasn't returning. Io continued to rub her belly, but she seemed like she wanted to tell me more.

"What are you going to do to at least stall his efforts?"

"Stall? We're going to kill him, and the others. No one's trying to buy time!" Azrael shouted at her, clearly frustrated.

Io jumped in shocked at his response, then looked at me for help. I shook my head and held my hands up.

"We literally have three days to figure something out," I said, unsure of myself.

"Zeus' brothers should probably be in his temple when you arrive. No question about that. But as far as what they can do…." Io said, looking sad, "You should probably do some research."

"We're going to blow them up," Nathan said walking in and glaring at Io, "Why should we concern ourselves with their powers?"

"When they're released, there's no telling how angry they'll be…" she continued.

"I thought they already were?" Azrael asked, biting into an apple, "Which is it?"

She was silent for a moment. Maybe she was mulling over how we already heard most of what she was telling us. Then she became teary eyed as she looked at me, then up at Azrael.

"Whatever you do, make sure he's dead," she whispered.

Sincerely, she was playing us up.

"Duly noted!" Nathan exclaimed.

For some reason, Io burst into tears. As I mentioned before, I had never been good with emotions. And it appeared I wasn't the only one. Azrael hit Nathan on the shoulder and shook his head, but looked at Io with aggravation. *Why was she crying*!

"It's been nice," Azrael said, helping her up, "But we have so much to do….and I'm sure you need to get back…"

He pushed her to the door as Nathan and I followed. Io looked surprised we were rushing her out, but it was true. We had a lot to do! She turned and stood in the frame of the door, tears still spilling from her pale face. She looked at me as if we were best friends, and I stole her boyfriend from her, then she looked at Nathan.

I never felt it was in Azrael's character to be sympathetic. Not even towards me. Sure he loved me, and he was scared for my safety…but I had a general opinion of men and emotions. To my surprise, he bent over enough to give Io a gentle hug. Then he nodded at her, and closed the door. Instead of the jealousy I was expecting, I too leaned into hug him. It had to be one the sweetest thing he's done since I've known him.

"Now back to business," he said, allowing me to linger by his side, "Have you come up with anything."

"No," I said, disappointed in myself, "It's not what it used to be."

Azrael stopped walking, and turned me so that I was facing him.

"Just because you're mortal doesn't mean you can't think of anything," he started off, "what's any different about now? You can't die of disease or perish from hunger."

Nathan smiled and sat down, staring at us.

"That was my gift as a goddess, I was more so strategic than the average male," I said, trying not to get upset, "All I am now is human, trying to stop a crazy angel and his band of fallen deities."

"It's simple, Enyo. What can you do to him that he hasn't already thought of?" he asked.

"Allow him to think he can get away with what he's doing…" I answered dryly.

"No seriously," Nathan said, smiling, "what if we let him think he can get away with it?"

Enyo seemed extremely frustrated with herself. A few days ago she was confident in what she might come up with. Now she seemed a little wary of her abilities.

"We wouldn't have the advantage, unless we're there once he's released from that table," Enyo said sadly, "it's the only way."

"He was angry when it happened, he'll be even more so once he's out," I mentioned, "We're probably die on sight."

"We can't wait for him at my father's temple, the Titans will be there," Enyo said,

"But…"

Nathan and I stared at her for a moment as she was hesitant to answer.

Enyo excused herself and went outside. This was a common reaction when the conversation became serious. I hope she didn't think we were truly dependent on her.

I followed her to the garage, then wrapped her into a hug. She was crying as she gasped a little for air. Her tears were seeping through my shirt, stinging as it mixed with the cold air. What do you say to someone who's lost everything?

"Enyo, we'll figure something out…."

"We won't," she said, her voice failing, "everything will be ruined…"

"Well it won't be your fault. It's my own. I should have acted when I found out what was going on…but…"

She wrung herself free and looked at me in anger. The light glistening off the snow allowed a hint of illumination, showing her gathered facial expressions.

"I thought you would die in Hades Hall. I truly didn't let it absorb until I realized I was falling."

"Don't ever let me hinder your emotions in such a conscientious decision. My hips aren't that much of a distraction," she spat.

"If it's sex I wanted, I would have gotten it by now," I retorted, "you couldn't seem to keep your hands off of me."

"Oh…so now I'm an easy piece of ass? What is it with you?" she said, straining her tone.

"I'm being honest with you. I had a million things going on in my mind. Saving you seemed to be the better option! Don't mock my empathy. I've never loved a woman like you before. At least not one worth my efforts…"

Enyo looked surprised at my response. She was used to fighting about her purpose, her body, her worth. Or was it a struggle all her life? Placing and disregarding her self in the mist of others selfishness. I was definitely out of her league if that was the case.

I leaned into to hug her again. Even if I reacted to Hades' news, there wasn't a thing that could have been done. Everything had been set in motion the minute I laid eyes on Enyo. Ever since then, I've had nothing but trouble.

That evening I was laying on the floor with Enyo again. Any other time I had laid on the floor, it didn't matter. I would be wide awake thinking about the last person I killed. The past few nights I've been sleeping as if I were drunk.

But tonight I could tell Enyo was extremely restless, so I shoved her slightly when she rolled over on her right side. She sat up, pressing her weight against the floor with her hands. Smiling at me, she laid on her left side.

Soon her hand was on my chest. Enyo made it seem as if her fingers were walking. She stopped in the middle, and maneuvered her fingers down to my stomach. Once she was near my belly button, I grabbed her hand and looked at her.

"Don't do that," I whispered, "even if I did let you do anything, I wouldn't know what to do."

"Why," she asked, grinning, "afraid you can't meet up to my standards?"

"I'm a virgin, Enyo…."

"Seriously?" she said, sitting up, still grinning, "but you're absolutely gorgeous."

She freed her hand from mine, then moved it slowly down my stomach again. I sat up and looked at her as if I meant to be serious, but she didn't pay it any mind. As soon as she reached the top hem of my underwear, the light flicked on. Ya Ya was standing with Nathan at the door way. Both were holding two large buckets. Nathan sat his down and tossed the blanket on my feet over my head.

"Well, now that we can't see any of that, let's get down to business…"

I pulled the blanket off and looked at Enyo, who was blushing, and smiling sheepishly. I had been exposed, and everyone was acting as if nothing happened.

"Ya Ya has made a larger portion of the Bella Donna and krythm mixture. But on our way back to Olympus we have to fly carefully. If any of this spills, it could be catastrophic," Nathan explained, "and very wasteful."

"So, what if it falls on someone here?" I asked out of curiosity.

"They'll die, by melting. If they're human….so let's be extra careful," he said, smiling a little, "I would hate to melt, and die…"

"Me too," Enyo added, nodding.

I smirked as I stood to walk towards one of the buckets. Then I looked at Ya Ya.

"Nathan went back to The Realm of the Forgotten and retrieved some more krythm, if you're curious," she said smiling at me.

I frowned at Nathan. I really wish he would have told me he had gone, but it probably didn't take him long.

"Did you see Elmer?" I asked.

He shook his head, and picked the buckets up by their handles, moving them to the back door in the kitchen.

"We'll let you two get back to sleep," Ya Ya said sweetly.

Nathan whirled around the corner, and before switching the light off, gave the gesture that he was watching us. I looked over at Enyo, who was still smiling as if she had no intent of anything Nathan would say. With the light off, I could still see her from the illuminating moon, shining through Ya Ya's skylight.

I looked up to see if I could spot it, when I felt Enyo's hand on my stomach again. Something in me wanted her to continue…*but*.

"You're fallen now," she whispered, tugging at my shirt, "how much trouble could we get in?"

"We're not married," I said softly, hoping it would change her mind, "I would like to commit to you before I do…"

I gasped at the touch of her hand. Then I closed my eyes and bit my lip. It amazed me that no matter what I said to her, she insisted to carry on with her actions. Enyo took my left hand and placed it on her right breast. I opened my eyes in wonder at the feeling; she was so soft, and warm. But I still wouldn't have any idea of what to do. So I scooted away, then laid on my left side and closed my eyes.

I heard her sigh, then lay down as well. This had nothing to do with marrying her. I didn't think it was a good idea. And now, I was laying on the floor, with my back turned to the most beautiful woman I had ever met. *And, I can guarantee most of the blood from my brain and body swarmed in one place right now.*

I tried to clear my mind of what we could do. How much fun it would be, how good it would feel, but nothing was helping. I rolled over on my back and saw her sitting up looking at me.

The moonlight set a spotlight for her beauty, which really got to me. It was just enough for me to sit up, lean in and kiss her. Soon, she had straddled herself on my lap, and my hands and her hands were everywhere. Once in a while, my lips would travel down to her neck to nibble.

She availed my actions, and scratch along my back or chest. Once I reached her lips to kiss again, she would moan softly and smile. I had gotten to the point of wanting to tear away her clothing, and take her right there on the floor. But she stopped, and looked at me, cheesing.

"I love you…" I whispered near her ear.

"I love you too…" she said softly.

Since we were both quiet, I made my hands busy by rubbing her back.

"Do you think you would appreciate me more if we waited," she said quietly.

"I want to make sure everything we have to do is done before we enjoy ourselves," I responded in confidence.

She sat up to smile at my remark, then buried her head into my chest. Nothing compared to holding her. Kissing her. Touching her. Nothing compared to her cuddling into me and listening to my heart beat.

I motioned to her I was laying back, but she came with me. Moving her hair out of my eyes, I noticed how steady her heart was beating. How calm she was. When I first met her, I assumed she was always in a bluster of emotions. Then I wondered if she had thought about me the first time I met her.

Soon my eyes were closed, and I could hear her steady breathing. I sat up to move her to my right side when a gentle knock came from the front door. Enyo was still asleep, and I waited a couple of minutes, when the knock came again.

Scurrying to stand, I noticed the snow blowing like crazy from the window. When I opened the door, I was surprised to find a little girl standing outside. She had on thick glasses, and was literally bundled from head to toe. I wasn't exactly sure what to say, so I stepped outside, shivering instantly to cold winter wind whipping by.

"How can I help you?" I asked her quietly.

"I need to speak with Whitney," she said smiling, "My name is Melissa."

Chapter 10: Athena's Other Family

Melissa and I sat at the table, still eye balling each other. I wasn't sure of what to say, but I didn't want her standing outside. It was, however, fortunate that I remembered the mortal name Enyo used for herself.

I stood to fetch some hot chocolate. But as I began rummaging for the milk in the fridge, I kept staring back at the strange child. She couldn't be older than 9, she was tiny, and she was breathing on her glasses and cleaning them with a dirty rag.

I pulled out a coffee mug and filled it to the brim with milk. Then I pulled out a sauce pot, pouring it in. After that I set the temperature on medium and turned my attention back to her.

"How do you know…um…Whitney?" I asked, with my arms crossed.

"She directs the chess tournaments at the rec center by my house," she said, "I haven't seen her in a while."

"So, you traveled to another state to find her?" I asked, suspicious of her story.

The smile she was sporting quickly faded. Then she looked around to see if anyone else was in the room.

"Your name is Melissa, you're about 9 years old, and your parents are…?" I asked, trying to get to the bottom of it.

"My father is dead, and mother is missing. So I came to the only place I was sure I'd be safe," she said, her voice cracking with emotion, "Can I use your restroom?"

I pointed her off into the right direction when I realized the milk had boiled over. As I cleaned my mess, I went over what the girl told me. *Something wasn't right.* With that thought, I went into the front room to shake Enyo awake. Once she sat up, she pushed off of me and cursed a little.

"What?!" she hissed, "I was asleep."

"A nine year old girl…by the name of Melissa is here for you…"

She opened her eyes and stood straight up to grab her pants. Once she secured them she followed me to the bathroom door to listen in on her. After pressing her ear on the cheap, thin plywood, she snapped her glare at me, attempting to pinch my shoulder.

"You let a strange 9 year old girl into the house!" she whispered, pinching me again, "have you seen *Children of the Corn* or the *Omen!*"

"Those are movies, woman!" I said, trying to put my hand over her mouth, "she asked for you by name anyway!"

The door opened slowly as Enyo and I gaped in shock. The little girl that entered the house transformed into a carbon copy image of Enyo.

"Athena!" Enyo exclaimed, embracing her into a hug.

She shot a glare at me, then walked her sister into the kitchen. I was still astounded that a little girl changed into an Enyo look alike in the bathroom. This made me wonder even more…Everything exciting happened in the bathroom. Teleportation. Changing your form. I wonder how much fun I could have in the bathroom. I studied the towels and shower curtain, but began to follow them to the kitchen.

"Azrael was trying to fool me, I guess. He said some girl I used to volunteer for during chess matches found me two states away," she joked, sitting down at the table.

"I am Melissa."

"HA!" I said, pointing in Enyo's face. She glared slightly and turned her attention back to her sister. "But that still confuses me…" I admitted.

I sat down at the other end of the table, hoping to hear a story.

"I've been living on earth, in secret for thousands of years. More so to watch you than anything. But my current family adopted me after finding me living in an alley by a restaurant. I had lost contact, as you can say, with you. But when I met them, everything got better…." She said smiling at Enyo.

Enyo looked completely stumped. She bit her bottom lip, then closed her eyes and rested her hands on her face. As she wiped the tears away, she looked back at her sister, smiling as well.

"These two years I've been watching you play chess, you've been watching me…" Enyo said quietly.

"Yes, you are my most beloved sister. I wouldn't have it any other way," Athena said, grabbing Enyo's hands, "I'm just glad to know you're alive."

Athena looked around for a moment, then back at Enyo and I.

"Where's Apollo?"

Nathan shuffled in, rubbing the sleep from his eyes. It was a growing trend…going over something important hours into the night.

"He's with April," Nathan answered, "they live together. I saw him when I went by A.Z's house. So he's fine."

"April is lesbian," I said, thinking back on everything she's told me.

"Either that, or you don't know how to read women," Athena said, smirking.

"April isn't lesbian…" Nathan said, frowning, "she has a preference."

"But…"

"Forget about it," Nathan said, sitting at the table as well, "Is there anything you can tell us about Zerachiel?"

"He wants the Titans to destroy everyone's temple except for mine, and Enyo's," she started off quietly.

"Why?" Enyo said eagerly.

"Because we're the only ones that bare a threat to him, sister," Athena said, frowning a little, "The goddess of war, the goddess of wisdom. He's afraid we're plotting something…"

"I'm not a goddess anymore," Enyo said, almost inaudible.

Athena didn't seem shocked by this but she leaned in a little closer to Enyo's face.

"That's why I'm here. So we can plan something together," she said smiling, "You can't do this alone. However I cannot travel back with you."

"Why," Nathan said, staring at her.

"I have to find Io. I have a few questions for her," she said, glaring a little.

Athena stood up, and pulled out three rolls of parchment. As she was sitting she stopped and smiled sheepishly at Nathan, then unrolled the first scroll. And how cute was that, he was watching her every move…

"Before Azrael trapped him into the Table of the Lost, he had an embankment built to ward off nosey female centaurs. He thought it worked to his advantage. Then he realized they pulled up the earth and filled the ditch so they could pass through. Moments before you reached their camp, he located their position, and told Oris, the male leader of the centaurs…" she continued.

"How could he see us?" I asked.

"Zeus' temple and Trident gives anyone the ability to see anything they want. A clear view on Olympus, a compromised view on Earth. Another perk Zerachiel gained with his alliance with our father…In the courtyard of Zeus' is what some would consider to be The View of the Living. But since our race no longer has followers, Zerachiel worked hard to turn it into The View of Deities. So they kept tabs on you, Enyo, me, and Apollo. And they were able to keep tabs on anyone in Olympus as well. This is part of the reason why Zerachiel got away with so much."

"What deities would he be able to view?" I asked.

"At first it was the only Angels on earth. He started to summon most of them in your line of work, but when the invitation went out, the majority of them refused. They said unless God Himself asked them to meet Zerachiel in Olympus, they weren't going to go. In order to get rid of Zeus, he had to go through the scrolls Elmer gave you to find the crimes against our father. That way he could pin them on Enyo, which prompted the job you agreed to. He knew it would take you a couple of days to put it all together, but he figured it was enough time to do what he had been trying to do for thousands of years," she said, stopping to take a breath, "You've only been doing your job for three thousand years, and too him you were completely ignorant of the history he had with the descendants of the fallen deities. However, as much effort as he put into watching everyone, he never thought he was being watched his self."

"Elmer helped him?" I asked, hoping the answer was no.

Athena firmly shook her head, then turned her affection to Enyo.

It didn't matter what Zerachiel thought he would get out of this. He was dealing with a double edge sword. Whether he realized his consequences for playing both sides of the fence was beyond me, but I had now found our advantage.

"He going to pretend he's Zeus once he's freed from that table," Enyo said, "there's our chance."

"That's exactly what I was thinking. If we can find a way to convince them otherwise, they'll destroy Zerachiel themselves," I added.

"But you still have to destroy them as well," Athena said, "this is what you do."

Athena started off by explaining how I should lure Zerachiel into our trap. She said I would most likely have to fight him in order for him to actually follow me. Pulling out a map, she began to show exactly where it was the Titans were resting in Zeus' palace. Then she began to explain the explosive components in our mixture. Once she finished that, we began to piece the rest together. Sheila had given us the golden flares to ignite our deadly mixture, which would cause what humans compare to as a atomic bomb. Our only issue was being caught in the combustion as it went off. That's when Athena stopped us.

"You won't be able to fly out," she said, shaking her head, " you'll need something to fly you out."

"A dragon," Enyo said, smiling at me.

She pushed me on the head and smiled at her sister.

"How can we get one, seriously," Nathan said, shaking his head, "a dragon?"

"Leave that to me," Athena said, "I'll need to take Enyo with me. She'll be the one that can fly him in and out. And…I realize you only have a few days left."

Enyo stood up quickly to retrieve the huge coat I loaned her when Athena stopped her.

"There's more," she said, looking at me.

"Like?" Nathan and I asked in unison.

"You'll need to place those buckets of that mixture where I've marked it," Athena said sternly.

"And what's Enyo going to do? Have the dragon light it on fire?" Nathan asked.

"No," Athena said, "she'll figure it out."

Everyone fell quiet after that. Athena was bossy but helpful. Then her and Enyo began to prepare for their trip. I didn't like I had no idea where Athena was taking her, because if anything happened to Enyo, I wouldn't be able to find her.

I went into Nathan's room to sit on his bed. Pressing my hands against my face, I attempted to crush the stress away. I was thankful Athena came up with a battle plan. Everything she pointed out began to make sense to us.

What I didn't like was that neither Nathan, Enyo, nor I could come up with anything *at all*. It was discouraging. I felt weaker than I had ever felt in my life. I was a fallen angel who could still fly. I was just about as useless as....

Enyo was standing in the door frame staring at me. She didn't smile, or speak. But she slowly walked over to me, straddled me, and kissed me. I was enveloped in the moment, but she broke the kiss and left without saying anything. I was left there, confused, as usual.

I didn't budge. I heard the front door close shut, and I still hadn't moved.

After ten minutes I came into the living room where Nathan was standing, looking up at his mother's skylight. I looked up with him, noticing how full the moon was, then fixed my gaze to Nathan and smiled a little.

"They teleported," Nathan said patting me on the back, "sometimes I wish I could do that instead of flying."

"Why?" I asked, looking at him in surprise.

"My skin becomes so chaffed and dry…" he said rubbing his left arm, frowning.

I pushed him by his head, attempting to get him onto the floor as I walked back into the kitchen. It was beyond me how Athena had spent thousands of years plotting to take Zerachiel down. And here sat two maps charting danger zones with where we would put our god destroying, explosive, human melting mix. I have to admit, I was still unsure of our odds.

Athena and I had traveled across the Atlantic to an isolated house on the Eastern edge of Russia, almost clipping the limits of Siberia. I was surprised to find she owned a small amount of estate, which was about three miles away from the next. As I walked through her house, I noted that most of it was empty except for her room, and the guest area. We went into her closet to change for the weather when I noticed on the back wall her carefully displayed golden bow and arrows.

I had wondered how long she had the house, but I was too tired to ask. As soon as I changed, I found myself cuddled in the guest bed, head into the pillows. She came next to me and began to rub my back as she used to when I was a child.

"You'll definitely need your rest. Tonight we have to fetch that dragon," she said softly, still rubbing.

"Where is he at?" I asked, looking back at her.

"The next house, about three or four miles from here. He's a Russian diplomat that has a lot of mistresses, so on and so forth. Let's just say if he doesn't, he's getting black mailed..."

I gave her a strained look as I mulled over what she told me.

"Wait," I said, ignoring the last bit of information, "There's a dragon in someone's house? Just all willy nilly like?"

"Yup."

It was hard to wrap my mind around the actual existence of a dragon. But Athena had never lied to me, so I went with my first instincts. I started to fall asleep, when I realized it was already dark. The wind outside howled as it lapped against the window, asking to come inside. I noticed Athena still sitting in the same spot she had been previous to my nap.

She tossed a handful of black clothes on my lap once I sat up. Then she smiled and turned on the light.

"We have to be incognito," she said, slipping off her own clothes, "and we can't teleport into the confinement where the dragon is being held, I don't want to startle him."

I nodded and began to change my clothes. Once I was dressed, I looked in the mirror and shook my head.

"I look like a Greek ninja…" I said in dismay.

She was wearing similar gear to mine, but the golden arrows and bow that once hung on her closet wall were now securely strapped to her back. Then she draped a huge brown cloak over herself. Soon we were out in the elements walking to her SUV. In the front was a huge snow plow, which made me raise my eyebrow at her *again*. She wasn't just pretending to be a little girl, she clearly had made herself comfortable all around the world.

Truly, the only issue I had with Athena was her lack of concern. She told Azrael and Nathan she knew where to find a dragon without mentioning we had to steal the dragon. It was sad to see this magnificent creature chained underneath the estate of a rich Russian diplomat. I shook my head at Athena as she began to pull her shawl off, then she handed me a chain.

"This guy owes me a favor, anyway," she said, smirking.

She secured her bow and arrows to her back again and looked at me.

"Where did you hide the chain….?" I questioned, surveying her.

She grinned, then began to sneak into the chamber. I followed after her, unsure of what I should be doing. Athena appeared out of the shadows and motioned me towards her. I began to tip toe when I realized the chain was clinking against itself. I rushed over to her as fast as I could, but I feared it was too late. *He began to move.*

"Um…Athena," I said, trying to keep my balance as the floor beneath us trembled, "Why were we the ones to retrieve him?"

"It's a male tendency to adhere to female command," she said in a snobbish manner.

The dragon began to stretch. From where he sat up, it was dark, but when his head hit the skylight of his confinement I could see he was bigger than I anticipated. Athena pulled me to run with her, and soon we were under him. She took the chain out of my hand and made a loop, then she began to twirl it around. She grunted as she thrust it up into the air. I was hesitant with this action, but it made its way back around to the other side.

Athena pulled down on it so that the dragon would lower his neck. The whole time I began to wonder why he was so tame. Once his head was closer I could see that his mouth had been welded shut except for a small opening. And from the little light in the room, the feeling in his eyes showed that he was tired of where he was.

I reached up to touch his chin but Athena secured the chain around his neck, and began to climb onto him. That's when the chatter of arriving voices came from the distance.

"Shhhhh, Aries," she said, petting him on his side, "You're coming with us."

Aries began to grunt and moan as he backed away from the front gate. I ran up to Athena's hand, then climb onto him, in front of her. I secured a hold on the chain and reared his head to back him up a little faster, when the lights in his chamber flicked on. Without thought, an arrow whizzed by, dropping the first man that stepped in. Then two more arrows followed, taking out the next two that entered.

"Aries, ascend!" I said, tugging at the chain.

He snapped his head back, and began to unfold his wings.

"Athena!" I screamed, looking up, "we have a huge…glass problem!"

"I see it!" she screamed back over the muffled roar of Aries, "once he's in flight, he'll start to ascend upward…"

"His mouth is welded shut!"

Athena took a couple of arrows and shot near his nostrils. The metal casing began to tumble off, as Aries continued to rise to the ceiling. Soon we were diagonal, and now was the perfect time for him to use his fire.

"Aries, the glass!" I screamed, hoping he would understand.

"Here it comes!" Athena warned me.

The surface of his scales heated up and in the blink of an eye, a huge fireball retracted from his jaws. I closed my eyes and covered my face as we flew through the hole. When I realized how high in the sky we were, I began to scream out of joy. Athena whooped for a moment, and turned to wave goodbye at Aries' now destroyed confinement.

"Direct him to go Southeast!" she yelled under the pressure of the wind, "we need to hit the Mediterranean before dawn so we won't be seen!"

"What does that do for us!" I shouted back.

She flicked me at my doubt in her advice, so I snapped the chains and tugged left for Aries to turn. As big as he was, he was gentle during flight, and obeyed my gesture. Athena began to tie my hair up in a bun, then she leaned into me, hugging above my waist.

I had never ridden a dragon before, and I've only seen one in my lifetime. *This was taking my breath away.* Without knowing how long it would take us to arrive to open water, I noticed a increase in the temperature. Soon I could smell the ocean, and feel the mist of it as we started flying lower.

Aries crashed into a wave, and groaned a little. He was flying ten or so feet above the water, and he began to slow his pace. I looked back at a drenched Athena and laughed at her face. I didn't mind the splash as much as she did. It was a while since I had done anything this thrilling. *Or had my whole life been nothing?*

I hesitantly reached down to rub him on his neck. Once I placed my hand on his scales, I could feel how warm he remained. He moaned slightly as I began to rub him a little harder, then I sat back and looked at Athena. She was smiling at me again.

"What?" I asked, tipping my head.

"I missed you. You have no idea how hard it was to keep all of that under wraps…."

"I'm actually relieved I put so much effort into getting to know that little girl. It helped so much," I told her, "You have no idea."

"So here's the issue," Athena said, interrupting me, "You'll be able teleport Aries in twelve hours. By the time you reach Giza, the stars should be just starting to show. The reason I want to do it then is because there is a time difference. It's going to take about 2 hours in Olympus, which is two days here."

"Isn't someone going to notice that we're riding on a huge dragon...." I said, petting Aries again.

"Not if we're in the air. Once we reach the Northern Delta for the Nile, we're going into hiding. He's flying low to give his self some rest. Besides, I have the perfect hiding spot."

"So when the stars come out, they'll be perfectly aligned?" I asked, still curious.

"Yes, which opens up the door between Olympus and this world," Athena continued, "the reason we're doing it right at dusk is to cut down on any spiritual transferences...."

I nodded, figuring I completely understood what she meant. If Zerachiel knew we were coming on a dragon, he'd probably fly up to meet us as soon as we entered Olympus' atmosphere. I shook my head a little at the thought of not defeating him. And I'm pretty sure I wasn't the only one who doubted this plan.

"I thought you weren't coming..." I asked, looking back at her again.

"I'm not," she said sadly," I have an appointment with Elmer."

"Oh," I said quietly.

Asking why probably wasn't the best idea. When it came to personal issues, Athena had a tendency to be stand offish. I nodded at her, then looked out into what seemed to be an endless ocean.

After a while, Aries was swimming with the top most of his body out in the open air. He was moving his large tail back and forth, and every now and then, he would sort of ride a oncoming wave.

Soon we were at the delta, but Athena took a hold of the chain, and guided us underground. I saw familiar artwork in the carvings of the granite rock as I followed Aries and Athena down the tunnel. I ran my hand across the wall, admiring everything I saw. Another fallen city in the mist of uncalculated power.

For most of the day we rested. Athena said she was going to a near by market to buy camels for Aries, as well as a harness. I questioned her about the harness and I asked if there was anywhere I could go without being noticed. She laughed at my question, but mentioned there was a pool in the middle of the buried ruins we had been camping in.

I walked through, feeling connected at once. All of the illustrations were amazing. It was weird to see drawings and inscriptions of later dated Greeks. Cleopatra's face was everywhere. If it wasn't Cleopatra's, it was Alexander's.

I waded my feet in the pool that had a weak excuse of a fountain. I started to close my eyes and relax, when I heard a strange noise.

"Hello?" I spoke, becoming a little wary, "is anyone there?"

"Where have you been?" I heard a familiar voice say.

The light coming from the crack in the ceiling started to reveal a mutated form. As soon as I could make it out, I noted that it was Randal. He smiled sadly, then moved closer.

"Yes," a female voice said, "we've missed you."

I looked behind Randal when I realized Rachel was standing in Randal's place.

"It just isn't the same," I heard Randal.

I stood up and nearly fell when they decided to stand to the side. Then the two split, forming their own bodies. Both of them smiled at me as if I would take this lightly. But instinctively, I screamed.

"Shhhh!" Rachel said, placing her hand over my mouth, "it's alright, we're not here to harm you!"

"Janus was killed thousands of years ago!" I said, still hysterical.

I pushed them off of me, then slipped into the pool. Feeling awkward and defeated, I stepped out, nearly falling on the slick granite floor.

"No, like a lot of other gods, we went into hiding," Rachel explained, "we found it was safer to live on earth, than on Olympus."

"We were following you, though," Randal said, cutting in.

"To give you the assurance of what's to come," Rachel said.

I eyeballed them, and I wondered if they knew how crazy that all sounded, then I sat down.

"I'm listening."

"You will defeat Zerachiel, and the Titans," Randal said.

"You will do all these great things, but you will almost lose your life. This includes your companion, Azrael," Rachel concluding.

She smiled, and I began to wonder if she realized she just told me I may die.

Yet...she was still smiling...

Randal came to me and patted my left shoulder.

"Without Athena, you would have failed," he said, making me feel worse.

"Gee, Randal...Thanks..."

"It wasn't to upset you. You sacrificed your immortality because it didn't prove another purpose to you. It wasn't a bad thing at all. But it doesn't hurt to get help."

"Trust me," Rachel said, coming behind him, "When I don't have Randal, I feel incomplete."

The two meshed back together, and disappeared into thin air.

Lovely. All I got from that was...blah blah blah, you'll win, blah blah blah, but you might die!

I found my way back to our resting spot, figuring Aries had finished devouring the camels. I nodded at Athena, then started to pack everything I had brought with me. Once I was done I patted on Aries, then pretended to adjust his harness when I turned to talk to her. She stood slowly, and handed me a map. Then she hugged me tightly.

"I don't know what's going to happen," she said, becoming choked up, "but I know you'll be successful in all that you will do."

"You say this like you're going to die, Athena," I said, becoming emotional as well.

"Even if I do, it's better than being the bastard child of a selfish god..."

I squeezed her tightly, but soon she unraveled herself from our hug, and bid Aries and I good bye.

I looked up into a near by crack, and noticed it was time for us to leave as well. I followed the instructions on the map, tunneling through the ruins, and ending up in Giza. I mounted Aries, and began to ascend into the clouds, where I could see below the three great pyramids.

Slowly, the stars geared into motion aligning with each other to form a gateway. I pulled on the chain to slow Aries down, then I waited for the portal to open. A small cord of lightening began to form in front of Aries and myself. Then it opened up, showing like a tear in the sky.

I snapped the chain for Aries to move forward, but he was as hesitant as I.

"We have to, Aries," I said sadly, "Do it for me, big guy."

He moaned a little, then slowly flew into this gap in time and space.

I wish the instructions on the map told me to hold my breath.

Chapter Eleven: Incedus

To me it seemed two days couldn't come fast enough. The closer it got, the more anxious I became. Nathan asked me to meditate with him, but that really wasn't my kind of thing. I am more so surprised to hear that this guy I've known for a few years was so…different.

There was one thing that seemed to stay on my mind, how long did April and Apollo know each other? Then I wondered if she knew he was a god. She isn't a stupid person, April's quite sharp, actually. So I decided to take a trip to work, seeing as how I hadn't been there in a while.

"April," I said quietly, walking into the back room.

"Azrael," she teased back.

When I turned the corner she smiled at me, and as usual, rested her hands on my shoulders.

"We need to talk," I said softly.

"Yes, we do," she agreed, "You go first."

"I'm the Archangel of Death?" I said, obviously unsure of my presentation.

"I knew that," April said, smiling, "I think what I'm about to tell you is far more interesting."

I frowned at her response.

"How could you have known that?" I asked, following her to the meat locker.

"Because I'm with Apollo," she said, turning to smile at me again.

"Because you're *with* Apollo?" I said, making sure I understood.

April was still smiling at me as if I had been a fool this whole entire time. We watched each other briefly then she sat down near the sink.

"How did you two meet?" I said, sitting next to her.

"I'm an Angel, Azrael," April said quietly, "how else do you suppose."

"I was under the impression you were into women…" I said, blushing a little, "shows how much I know."

"Maybe you look too deep into your disconnection from women. You stuck to the laws of heaven, so you couldn't tell a harlot from your wife, in my honest opinion."

I couldn't disagree with what she said.

"Were you watching me?" I asked, looking at her again.

"Enough to make sure you were okay, but it wasn't a task of mine."

April started off with the story on how she met Apollo. How they decided not to marry, but went ahead and had children. I paused and looked at her in confusion.

"Aren't you fallen?" I question, hoping the answer was yes.

"No…"

Of course not!

"So why did I fall?"

"Perhaps to insure the completion of your task? Just because you've been cast out of heaven doesn't mean you're not needed. You may not have fallen for the reason you think you fell anyway. I'm not a Messenger Angel, or an Archangel of Death. I was created to give Him praise. I've been doing it for thousands of years…"

"Yes, but you slept with Apollo, and…" I said, raising an eyebrow.

"That isn't the most unforgivable sin. You fell probably to show you there's more to life than always finishing a job. You may have fell because this is your last assignment, and it was always your assignment. You also might have fallen so you could be with Enyo, and it encouraged her to sacrifice her immortality as well. Everything happens for a reason," she explained, "it was never because you weren't good enough. The fact that you are still obedient should bear witness to your life."

"So…is Apollo actually a god still?" I asked, already thinking of an answer.

"He sacrificed his immortality way before he bumped into me. So he's just been human, actually. No one realized it."

"How was he traveling back and forth from here to Olympus?"

"Nathan, Hermes, sometimes Athena…sometimes me. He was there enough to be known, but he didn't care too much for his relations. He could also keep an eye on Athena and her family, as well as Enyo."

"We have to defeat Zerachiel," I said, changing the topic, "otherwise we can kiss this world good bye."

"He can't reign on earth, or bring his campaign here. That's why he's on Olympus. But you don't get away with anything, trust that," she said standing up, " and as fearful as you all are, he's set his self up to fail."

"He released the Titans, so it's not just him…And I don't believe he'd just stop there. Why put all that effort into it….One of our main concerns lies with telling the Titans the truth."

She smiled at me, and patted my hand.

"They weren't born yesterday, hun."

I felt a stream of confidence run through me that I hadn't felt in a while. I smiled back and stood to leave.

Before I decided to ascend, I wandered by my house to see if it was still standing. I stared in shock that the roof had be torn off. Or burned off. It was hard to tell which happened first.

The tree that Hermes used to perch in was completely destroyed as well. My neighbor saw me standing outside gawking at my discovery, and felt it was necessary to come talk to me.

"It was so strange," she started off, opening her destroyed picket fence, "it was snowing real bad, then out of no where, a lightening bolt struck the top of the house…"

"Lightening during a snow storm? I'm sure there's another reason…" I said, raising my eyebrows at her.

"Well, what do you think happened?" she said, moving a little closer.

"Someone was attempting to take my life."

She didn't say much after that remark. She stood there shivering, then complained about being cold, and made her way back to house. I could tell from the damage that Zerachiel had targeted my house at some point, in the hopes I would be inside. What I didn't understand is why he couldn't tell if I was inside or not.

After surveying my last home for a little bit longer, I walked back to the store, then to the back. I looked to see if anyone could see me, and I ascended. Once I landed in Ya Ya's front room, I could see Nathan sitting on the weathered couch, smiling.

"I saw Athena," he said once I sat next to him.

I smiled at his announcement, and gestured to him for more information.

"I will never know why after thousands of years I was a virgin. Ever," he said, expressing himself with his hands, "I had wondered what I was missing in this world…"

"Look," I said in humor, but not wanting him to continue, "just say it was everything you anticipated and leave it at that….but where is she now?"

"She went to find Io, and she said she had an appointment with Elmer."

Frowning slightly, I stood in retreat to the fridge. It got more affection from me than anyone. Even if I was a fallen angel, I still had an appetite. I bit into an apple when I saw Nathan smiling at me again.

"I think I love her…" he said childishly, melting into his stool, "she's awesome. And…"

I held my hand up, unsure of what details I might hear, then I tossed an apple at him.

"When should we leave?" I said, polishing off another apple.

"Tomorrow afternoon…" he said, literally swallowing the apple whole.

I stopped chewing for a moment and stared at him in astonishment. Then I laughed a little and shook my head at him.

"It's just an apple!" I exclaimed, tossing him another.

"I need the energy. Athena took a lot out of me…"

I pushed the apple into his mouth then stood back. He blinked and took a huge bite and pulled it from his mouth.

"I get it," he said, in between munching, "No details."

"Why are we leaving early?" I asked, giving him the side eye.

"We have to set up those containers where Athena has it marked on the map," he answered.

"Exactly and approximately?" I said, frowning.

He shrugged, and finished the rest of his apple while standing up.

"We have to take our time with these," he said, pointing to the back door, "and we have the flares as well."

"Those buckets are pretty heavy. We don't want any melting humans."

Nathan stopped what he was doing and smirked at me like a child.

"If that happened, I'm sure it would cause me to become fallen as well," he said shaking his head, "there's always a 50/50 thing. It kills evil Angels, but acts as acid."

"We should give it some sort of name…" I said, indulging in his joke, "Oops."

Nathan roared out in laughter and clapped his hands on my shoulders.

"That's, my friend, is epic."

He walked away wiping the tears of his comedy off his face. Then he returned with chains and ropes.

"I know you had a lot of fun with Athena, but I'm not into that kind of thing…"

He stopped, as if he had an epiphany, then he looked at me and grinned.

"It's to secure the 'oops' to us, but thanks for that idea" he said, allowing the jumble in his hands to fall to the floor.

"So if I fall out of the sky, I die along with several hundred other people?"

He stopped again, but his face seemed a little more serious.

"When have you fallen out of the sky, all random like, during flight?"

I stopped to think but shook my head when I Ya Ya entering the room in a huff. She rummaged through the pantry for a moment, then pulled out a longer silver canoe like figure.

"Is that a gondola?" I asked, reaching out to touch it.

She nodded, and pulled out a piece of dark blue chalk.

"Mark your coordinates for where this mixture shall be placed. Then mark it on the silver gondola. When you're done, I'll recite a transporting spell to get it there faster. Safer. And oops free…" she said, eyeing Nathan.

Nathan seemed ashamed when she looked between the two of us. And with that, I sat down with a map of the world, and Athena's map. After taking the chalk from Ya Ya, I began to mark the coordinates as she explained. Then I marked them on the gondola. She examined my work and shook her head.

"You need to use constellations, not degrees associated with longitude and latitude. You'll end up sending it some where on earth. So which constellations are assembled in the night during the winter time?" she said, looking at Nathan, "you of all people should know this."

"Orion, Canis Major, and Canis Minor…Crater…Hydra…and…Lynx…" Nathan mumbled.

"Mark it down with the others you know of," she spoke to him.

Nathan wiped away my markings, and put down his own, first on the map. Then he did the same for the gondola. Ya Ya went into the pantry one more time, and pulled out 4 small barrels. Nathan marked those as well, then set them inside the gondola.

"Can you do that with food?" I asked her.

She laughed a little than shook her head.

"If you dropped a sandwich, it wouldn't kill anyone," Ya Ya replied.

"Depends on the sandwich," Nathan whispered.

She smacked the back of his head, and smiled at me.

We both nodded as Ya Ya turned into her kitchen and began fixing food for us.

"You have to eat here," she said softly, "you won't have time to think while you're there. And one more thing…"

"Yes, Ya Ya," Nathan said, sounding like a little kid.

"I'll have to get you there as I am doing your weapons."

I looked at Nathan as if she had gone crazy, then I fixed my gaze on Ya Ya.

"I see your replica for the barrels. But you have silver mini replicas of us?"

"No," she said, assembling another plate of sandwiches, "I have a map in my basement. All I have to do is mark the coordinates on your heads, and you'll travel there in the blink of an eye."

I didn't like the idea she was using a spell to transport us, but I felt we had no other choice.

After our meal, she had us pour olive oil on our heads. Then she used a butter knife and scraped off what she considered dirty.

Ya Ya then pulled out another piece of dark blue chalk and began writing on Nathan's forehead. And of course, I couldn't read what it said. She pulled me aside as well, and wrote on my forehead.

"It's not permanent, but it needs to sit for a while," she said, fanning at my head, "I'll transport you, Nathan, near where the concoction will be, and Azrael, you'll be transported into Hades' Hall."

We both nodded then stared at each other's foreheads.

"If this doesn't wash off," I said, staring at his, "I'm growing my hair out in the front."

"Can I borrow yours from the back, since its fairly long to begin with…"

"As long as you don't touch the hair in the front, my friend, you can do what you want with the back…"

Ya Ya was staring at us with her eyebrow raised. She shook her head then pulled Nathan onto the living room floor.

"Meditate on what you need to do," she said, pulling me to sit with him, "open your mind to positive energy. Allow the aura of contentment to flow."

I expected Nathan to hum. I peered through my long lashes, but Ya Ya flicked my nose. As I tried to ignore the paid, I close my eyes again. I wasn't sure how one meditated, but Nathan was completely silent. I did notice he had a pattern of breathing, but it was gentle and not labored. So I practiced these rhythmic breaths.

Soon I couldn't hear anything, but I had a clear view of the table Zerachiel was trapped in. I was calm, which was highly unexpected, and I was ready for whatever might happen. The table had been still, but it began to shake violently. Then I could feel the vibrations from the table under my feet…

Ya Ya was shaking my shoulder. I snapped out of my trance and smiled up at her.

"That was good, for your first time," she said softly, "let's go."

All the apprehension I had been feeling in the last few days was no longer present. After I dressed my self, and secured a few golden flares to my sides and back, I stood with Nathan on her astrological grid in the basement. I swayed a little once I looked down to see what I was standing on. I couldn't make out the readings, but…I also couldn't stop staring.

The constellations would give off a soft glow with every breath I took. But it made sense, Nathan and I were Angels. We had a direct connection to the universe. I looked to Nathan who was smiling at me and reaching out for a fist pump. I returned his gesture and nodded, then looked to Ya Ya.

"There isn't much for me to say," she said, standing before Nathan, "*Incedus*."

In wisp of dark blue smoke, Nathan vanished before my eyes.

Oh no, I'm not nervous at all, Nathan just disappeared!

Ya Ya came over to me, smiling as wide as I had ever seen her do before.

"*Incedus*."

Chapter Twelve: Fallen for a Purpose

Vomiting once more on the floor, I sat back on the dismounted wall holding my stomach. Maybe my arrival was a little too fast. And now wasn't the time to be sick. The light hit the table just enough to scare the shit out of me.

There, Zerachiel's wings were still frozen like stone right before my eyes. I took a couple of deep breaths and wondered if I should travel to find water. If only that were possible…the sound of approaching hooves echoed down the corridor..

Knowing I didn't have a chance of defeating them gave me a sprit of energy as I stood. I need a weapon. A sword, a bow with arrows, even a stone. As I walked down the dark purple stained hall, I peered into each room I passed, coming up empty every time.

I came across a chamber that was strange even after all the weird things I've seen. First, it was completely under water. Second, there were three absolutely gorgeous woman sitting aimlessly on a rock. As soon as the first stood up, I ran off. I wasn't too sure what that was about.

The next room was of no use as well. Nothing but books, but I had wondered if the severed arm on the floor could provide a decent defense. I ran down the hall once more, sure I would be intercepted when I passed a room full of weapons. The minute I entered, the door slammed shut. To my dreary surprise, the three women I had encountered before were in there.

"You know," the dark haired one started as she came closer, "men usually stick around when it comes to us."

"I can…er…I mean I can't think of why anyone wouldn't," I said, trying to think of which legend these women were from…

She stood under me, attempting to trace her hands up my frame. I smiled as I bit my lip and nodded my head.

"What can I say," I said, back up against the wall, "who doesn't love a siren…lurking around the underworld."

"Exactly," the others said.

"Exactly…" I agreed, palming the wall.

I pulled the sword on my hand out and swiped, cutting her on the shoulder. She fell to her knees, grasping her wound as I bolted to the door. The other two were apprehensive to attack, and allowed me to exit the room. Or maybe it was because a huge male centaur was standing outside.

I attempted to run past him, but he was keeping my pace. As soon as the ceiling in the hall began to mold into an dome, I elevated my self in flight, and circled around that area, trying to think of a way to attack him.

I flew in and swiped, then flew off. *Got him*. But it didn't seem like it did much, as he was still standing his ground. I flew lower again and took another chance with my sword, but he caught me off guard, and knocked me in my chest. I heaved back, flying through a closed door, and tumbling into a room.

I rose slowly, wary of my movements when his large hand caught me around my neck. He held me up against a pillar and smiled as he watched me choke. I attempted to strike him on his shoulder with as much force as I could muster, but nothing seemed to do the trick.

His grip tightened as I fought to pull his fingers from my neck. I gasped, gagging to breathe when I noticed a familiar silhouette.

Looking up I could see Nathan spiraling down with a spear in his hand. Everything seemed to be in slow motion at this point, and I was grateful he found me.

Nathan drilled in, grunting as he pierced the centaur's side with his spear. He landed on his back, pulled it out, then stabbed him in the back of his head. I fell onto the floor and began coughing and gasping for air.

"You're supposed to be at Zeus' temple!" I exclaimed, still fighting for air.

"Ya Ya had me land in Enyo's temple because she knew if I landed at Zeus', I'd probably be dead. Or I'd blow everything up..."

He helped me stand, then handed me my sword.

"I also saw a few straggling centaurs, and figured you might need some help," he said smiling.

"I have to go back to that table," I told him, holding on to his shoulder, "You need to spare you energy for the fight we have waiting for us at the temple."

He nodded, then took off. I watched him, then made my way back down to Hades' Hall. Everything seemed to *not* be going my way. In fact, I completely forgot the time difference between Olympus and Earth.

As the table began to creak and shake, I could hear the faint roar of Zerachiel coming from it. You could feel the floor beginning to tremble as if an earthquake were happening. I backed up, unsure of his arrival point with me once he was released.

A dark, red beam shot up from the middle of the table, and Zerachiel began to flex his wings. In anticipation for the fight, I felt like running. To be frank, I wasn't sure if I was going to be able to lure him to where I need to. But I fixed my stance, took a deep breath, and readied my sword.

The table burst apart, black wood pieces flying everywhere while Zerachiel stunted into the air. A huge gush of wind followed behind him, whipping the hair out of my face. He levitated as if he were relaxed while stretching his wings, and as soon as he spotted me he darted in my direction.

I ascended into the air as fast as I could, forgetting to secure my sword. Ignoring that it fell, I steadied my pace to exit. The halls twisted and turned making it nearly impossible to keep at least a body's length away from Zerachiel.

Once I was cleared out of the exit, I hustled the strength in my wings a tad more, just so I could stay alive. Aviating down, I began to search for a safe place to land when Zerachiel caught up with me. He tackled me in mid air and both of us came crashing into Aphrodite's temple.

I stopped short of a pillar, then stood up quickly so as not to be caught off guard. I stumbled a little when I realized I stepped on a hand. I swept to clear the fog at my feet, then I frowned at my discovery.

And there she was, I could see the dark purple decay growing and emanating from her body. Her hands were cupped around her stomach as if her womb had been filled. However, I could not spot Zerachiel. Because the fog had crept into the temple, it made it nearly impossible to see.

"I'm through with these games, I'm going to kill you!" I heard Zerachiel roar.

"As long as you die first!" I yelled back.

"I will never!" he hissed.

Nervous he would come from behind, I turned back and forth frantically, hoping to catch him first. I stopped moving and I could tell he was closer, but I couldn't point out where he was. A pocket of fog wisped into the air and as I looked up I saw he was flying downward in my direction. I ran and took off, dodging some of the pillars, making near misses each time.

Darting upward, I felt the fog swirled under feet, the weight of the mist making it harder to fly. As soon as I saw him coming after me, I geared my aviation towards him. We collided, but I kept my balance in the air. I began pushing him by his shoulder towards the ground, hoping this would be my last offense.

He pulled his knee up into my stomach, and pried me off of him. And right before I ended up in a pond, I swooped over it, then into the air again. He was glaring at me, with his fists clinched. It seemed this was a typical stance for him. Zerachiel was beginning to look like a child who never got his way. This was the ultimate temper tantrum.

In my mind, injuring him wasn't going to do anything but anger him even more so. And it was probably best to spare my energy as well. But perhaps I spoke too soon. Spears began shooting from below, and since the fog cleared, I could see a small handful of centaurs on the ground.

I evaded most of them, but the last one nearly cut me from navel to neck. I flew towards Zerachiel, attempting to cause a diversion. And once I was nearly neck and neck with him, my plan worked. Elusive to a few more spears, I noticed one caught him and clipped his shoulder.

"Not me!" he growled, throwing it back down.

It went into the chest of a centaur, killing him on impact.

Fatigue began to creep upon me, and I wanted more than ever to lure him into his fate. I began to fly in the direction of Zeus' temple, and I could feel the chase was on once more. I looped around, diverting my angle so that Zerachiel would follow.

The more I darted around, the angrier he became. I flew by Zeus' temple twice, but my last time flying around lead to Zerachiel almost catching me. The pressure from his wings seemed as though it would knock me out of the sky. But I kept my pursuit, and began to lower so I could land. I came in softly, but he split the floor to the entry way.

"Enough!" he growled under his breath.

We both stopped and stared as five very large frames began making their way to us. The first had similar features to Zeus, but he was much, much taller. As the others followed behind him, I realized neither of them paid me any mind.

"Who are you?" he said, his voice vibrating the air around us, "and where is my brother?"

"I am your brother…" Zerachiel said, his voice nearly failing him.

The tallest took Zerachiel by his throat, and threw him into a pillar as if he were nothing but a rag doll. I had vanished into the next chamber where I saw Nathan kneeling down.

"They nearly killed me!" he whispered in anger, "but I explained to them what happened, and showed him Zeus' corpse…."

"Shhh," I directed to him, "Zerachiel is talking."

I couldn't hear what he was saying, but Zerachiel sounded as if he was begging for his life. Soon it fell silent, then Zerachiel began to sob.

I peeked from behind the pillar to see what was happening. But I couldn't see much since they were surrounding him on all sides. Once the one closest to me moved, I jumped back and covered my mouth. They had pulled the wings off of Zerachiel's back, and left him on the floor in a bloody mess. He was laying on his side, but from what I could tell he was still alive.

"What is it?" Nathan said, reacting to my facial expression.

"They've plucked his wings as if it were nothing..."

"Perhaps you should be next..."

The air reverberated from the sound of his voice. Both Nathan and I exchanged uneasy glances, and shot up into the air as fast as we could. Once we were high enough into the atmosphere, I looked at Nathan, showing my fear.

"They did it as of he were a little bug!" I exclaimed.

"Did you see how big they...shit...wait!" he said looking down, "they're knocking one of those barrels over!"

He put his hand out in front of me, and pushed me back a little.

"You'll die."

"Do you supposed they know what it is?" I asked, frustrated.

A loud roaring came from below. Once of the titans fell to his hands and knees, screaming out for help. But soon his body began to melt into the marble. His brothers watched in horror, then looked up to the sky. One ran out into the garden, and pulled a tree up from its roots. Then he flung it towards us. As we evaded it, he scooped up a pillar, and threw it up at Nathan, who teed off of it, and flew a little higher. He came by my side, hesitant to fly down.

"We..."

"Are totally fucked?!" I said, looking at him in anger.

Soon the other brothers began to follow suit. Throwing pieces of the roof and pillars, trees, and marble at us. Nathan seemed to be okay, but I was feeling tired once again. I started to look around to see if I could spot Enyo, but it seemed she hadn't made it yet. We began to fly away, hoping to scope a better advantage. I stalled at this point, sure that Nathan would follow my lead.

The shortest one started bolting marble in the air, and igniting it with his finger tips. My eyes widened at this display of black fire, and I maneuvered along with Nathan to stay alive. He stopped as if he were resting, but his eyes were darting back and forth. The tallest one stood on the remains of the roof, and began to swing what seemed to be a sling shot. This is when Nathan decided he was going to fly down.

"He's following your every move, just stay where you are!"

"What?!" Nathan called out turning around.

A net sprawled out in the air, capturing Nathan. As the ties lapped around, it brought him down onto the ground. As a large cloud of dust sprung up where he landed, I could hear him groaning in pain. Another brother followed the previous action, so I waited for the net to fly into the sky. Just as it did, a fireball from no where turned it into ash in mid air.

Enyo had finally made it!

"Get on!" she yelled, nearing the dragon to me.

I climbed on, fearful of my life, then hugged on to her.

"Make sure to aim his fire away from the floor!" I yelled, "they spilled one of those canisters!"

"Not the brightest, bunch, are they?"

"No, to be honest."

She guided the dragon near Zeus' temple, then reared his head back.

"Fire, Aries!"

As we swooped by, a large fireball caught the smallest Titan. He flew off into the grass on the right side of the temple.

"He's looks to be unconscious for the moment, where are the others?" she asked.

Another Titan jumped out in front of us, slamming his fist onto the ground, up heaving the marble below. Enyo, yanked on the chain, pulling Aries almost straight up into the air.

"C'mon on Aries!" she said, tugging the chain to turn.

Soon we were flying downward, and Enyo ordered him to fire again, hitting a tree.

"Enyo, be careful!" I screamed, "You're going to kill us!"

"I'm going to lower you to get Nathan, and I want you to fly to the summit near the hills!" she yelled back.

"I'm not leaving you!" I bellowed.

I jumped off of Aries and grabbed a sliver of marble. Then I began cutting at the net. I could see Nathan was hurt pretty bad so I threw him on my shoulder, and moved back to Aries as fast as I could. To my surprise, Enyo was waiting when I came into the temple.

"Strap him in the back, and help me move these containers close to each other!" she yelled.

The floor began to shake, which made Aries fire off again.

"Aries, no!" Enyo screamed, running towards him, "Not until I say!"

He moaned slightly, tilting his head back and forth.

After securing Nathan, I ran over to the other side and began to drag our concoction to the middle. Then I retrieved another pail, sitting it next to Enyo's. We quickly flipped the lids off and began sprinting to Aries.

"Let's go!" she screamed.

A large foot kicked Enyo to the entrance of her father's temple. In my efforts to catch her, my wailing hand drew back as the other clasped the chain attached to Aries' neck.

"A bitch of a goddess," he roared, laughing out loud, "what a waste of flesh."

He began to pursue her as Enyo scooted back into a corner. She nodded at me, and gestured that I flew off. As soon as I snapped Aries' chain, he growled at me.

"Hey!" I yelled, getting on top, "I don't like you either, but we have to get her, so let's go!"

He started to ascend, when a large fireball came in our direction. I pulled his chains to avert the flames, and it was fortunate he was quick. Then we went into the air to circle around and save Enyo.

"Come on, Aries!" I yelled again, "I know you can move faster than that!"

He began to spin downward in Enyo's direction, and when he was close enough, he shot out a blaze towards the pursuing giant. To my surprise, the tallest began to scoop up a handful from the burning tree while throwing it towards us. But, Aries maneuvered out of the way with the greatest of ease. We swooped down once more to retrieve Enyo when I had an idea.

"I know you may not understand me, but I'm going to jump off to save her. Circle around to spare your life, and fly back to get us!"

He moaned a little, and I was almost sure…he didn't understand a thing I said.

But I refused to let her die.

When Aries was close enough, I jumped off, and rolled, landing next to Enyo. Then I began to open up my wings when a large piece of marble came hurling in my direction. I turned my back towards it, while covering Enyo in the corner.

"You have to go," she said, watching Aries fly up into the air.

"I can't leave the only woman I'll ever love!"

She grinned at me as I scooped her up to my chest.

"I always thought Angels were abominations," Zeus' look alike said, walking closer.

"Said the abomination!" I retorted.

And then I began to ascend. As I spiraled up and met with Aries, I could feel the heat from a fire ball at my feet. I placed Enyo next to Nathan, and without time to secure her, I aviated higher, reaching the outermost layer in the sky, nearing the heavens. I growled at my tired muscles, which were aching all over. I didn't have another option. So I fought against the pain.

Once I was sure the fireball dissolved into the atmosphere. I halted to divert my flight. Squinting my eyes through the specks of dust still floating up high, I made my way to Aries.

"Where are the golden flares!" I screamed to Enyo.

"The must have fallen off during flight!" she yelled back.

I felt around my back, and hip only finding one.

"This is it!" I said, looking at her.

She nodded in confirmation, though she appeared worried.

I seated myself forward and snapped on Aries chains.

"I need to fly over head, big guy!" I stated to him, "and once I light this flare and throw it, we have to go!"

He growled in affirmation, and swooped around to get a better angle. As we began to head inwards, a fireball rumbled to us. This time, Aries couldn't avoid being struck. Enyo sat up to pat out the fire, then she rubbed his side to calm him down. I jerked the chain to move to the left, then down.

Aries obeyed my directions and began to dart towards the temple.

"AZRAEL!" Enyo screamed out in fear, "You're too close, we'll never make it!"

"Yes we will!" I said, pulling the flare out.

I pulled the cord, and right as we passed over, I dropped it. Then I snatched Aries' chain upward to ascend again.

"Come on Aries!" I roared, "you have to fly faster!"

"Azrael!" Enyo, grabbing at my back to hold on.

"We'll be fine!"

"There isn't another portal!"

I cursed as I snapped Aries chain once more. The view from below was frightening. Everything was being engulfed in a tremendous white fire. It took no time to spread as it began to swallow Olympus whole.

As we neared the inner most part of the atmosphere, I took into consideration what Enyo had said. But as soon as I began to doubt we would make it, a strip of lightening appeared and began to peel apart, revealing a passage way.

I directed Aries to fly right, leading to the portal when I started to feel the hot fire lapping on his sides. He roared out in pain, but continued his pace, and soon it appeared as if the portal it self became engulfed in flames as well.

I could feel Enyo finger tips sinking deeper and deeper into my flesh as I looked back at an unconscious Nathan. This white fire had surrounded us completely, and it seemed we weren't going to make it. I looked back at Enyo and I could see her eyes were closed tightly.

The heat from the fire burned the surface of my skin, and I could feel how dry and brittle her hair had become as it whipped into my eyes. Clearing it to embrace her, I lapped my chin on Enyo's shoulder, then glanced at Nathan, hoping he was still tied down.

This wasn't how I wanted to die, but Enyo was with me. At least we'd still be together..

Funny. I lived for thousands of years, loveless, almost hopeless. And as death crept slowly upon us, I finally had a reason to live.

Enyo.

Nathan and I stood above Azrael's bed, smiling down at him. He had been sleep for five days, but we were sure he was alive. From time to time, he would snore loudly, waking us up out of our own sleep. Or he would mumble he was hungry, and no one could have his sandwich.

I held onto my stomach, still feeling the agony from being punted. There wasn't enough pain medication in the world. But Azrael endured further injuries than I could ever imagine.

Nathan patted me on my back as I sat down next to him, running my hand through his black curls. I wonder what he was thinking, and I wonder if he knew we succeeded. And as usual, he was completely unscathed. Not a single burn. Scratch, scrap. As good as new.

I felt his hand travel up to the one on my lap. He rolled over on his side and squeezed it slightly, then he brought it up to his lips and kissed it.

"I was sure that's what hell felt like," he said smiling a little with his eyes still closed, "but I'm sure it isn't a beautiful as embracing the love of your life."

"We all thought it was over," I said, kissing his forehead, "I shouldn't have doubted you."

He frowned, then opened his eyes, looking into mine.

"If I would have died holding you, I would have felt I lived my life *completed*."

He sat up, cupping my face near his while kissing me. Then he grimaced, holding his left side. I helped him lay down. Then I sat on his bed, still looking into his beautiful blue eyes.

"Did you take me to an E.R. or hospital or something?" he said looking around.

"No," I answered, looking out of the window, "This is one of Apollo's homes."

He sat up again and looked out of the window.

"How long was I asleep?" he asked out of confusion.

"Five days. We made it through the portal, and crash landed onto the sand in Giza," I started to explain, "Apollo and Athena were there to intercept us."

"I thought Athena had a meeting with…"

"She did…" I told him, "it didn't take as long. In fact she was up and atom within thirty minutes."

"And did she find Io?"

I fell silent, unsure of what to tell him. We still needed to find her, but I didn't want to spoil our victory. So I smiled sweetly and stood up to open the curtain on the other side of the room.

Azrael sat up once more and began grinning.

"We're in Hawaii, aren't we?"

"Puerto Rico, but close," I answered.

He nodded at this information, his face remaining pleasant.

"So when are we having kids?" he asked, watching me sit down again.

I blinked at him, then rubbed my belly for a moment, imitating Io.

"Do you see this body?" I said.

"I mean," he started off, "you're…okay. I can understand if it were my body…."

I laughed at him, and pushed him in his head.

"We'll know once we're ready," I said, "besides, you still have the challenge of pleasing me."

He raised his eyebrow at me and looked me up and down. Then he grinned like a fool.

"How hard could that be? You've had your hands all over it..."

I scoffed and stood up, but he pulled me back down onto his bed. He was still smiling at me, even though I knew he was in pain. I kissed his forehead once more then rubbed my nose into his. His eyes closed but he was smiling from ear to ear.

"I love you, Enyo," he said softly.

"I love you too, Azrael," I said, "even if you are an Angel."

He chuckled a little then kissed my lips. Snuggling into his pillow he grimaced once more as he rubbed my back.

"You did it," Nathan said, walking back in, "I can't believe we're alive."

Azrael was quiet now, but with his eyes were closed he continued to grin.

"How dare you doubt my skills," he retorted softly.

Nathan chucked a pillow onto his face and crossed his arms.

"Well," Nathan began, "Thanks for the support. I helped you!"

"A lot," Azrael said, pushing the pillow on the floor, "Without you, I wouldn't be here. None of us would."

Nathan seemed pleased with his reply and stepped closer to the bed.

"Athena made a huge meal for all of us, and she said it's just about ready. I came to get you guys…."

With that I helped Azrael stand, then I helped him dress. We walked slowly down the hall to the dining room, and as soon as we turned the corner, the room burst into applause. Hera, my mother was present. She promised to explain how she escaped the chaos…later.

Then there was Apollo, Hermes, Athena, April, and of course Nathan. I turned to clap as well, then I bowed and smiled.

Azrael was teary eyed, but smirking. I could tell he was thankful for the adulation he was receiving. Apollo moved to help him sit, then he gestured everyone raise their glasses.

"You conquered a crazy Angel. You killed the first descendants while bringing my beloved sister back alive, and…you erased the stigma we once carried on our backs," Apollo said, smiling at him, "To Azrael."

"To Azrael!" we all said in unison.

He was beaming, it was good to see he was confident in himself. I was glad to be alive, and glad that what I used to call home was now gone….forever. I nodded at everyone that came up to pat him on the shoulder or shake his hand. He was happy, finally. At peace, smiling. Ever so calm.

Everyone took their seats, and began passing platters back and forth. I distracted myself from the clatter of spoons and forks and jubilant conversation. All of our efforts might have been foiled, to say the least.

Through all the laughter, and praises he was receiving I couldn't help but wonder one horrible thing.....

Did Io indeed hold Zerachiel's seed?

Epilogue: Elmer's Letter to Nathan

Dear Nathan,

It is your old friend, Elmer. I have a few points before I become congratulatory.

First I would like to point out that although Enyo and Athena have taken a half dose of krythm, they will still live thousands of years. It's complicated and too scientific to explain right now. Once you all are well rested, I'll pull you, Azrael, and Apollo aside, explaining, thoroughly, the side effects. But as a precaution, if either lose mass amounts of blood, they will die. They're blood can be considered unique, and cannot be replaced unless you find another like them.

I am so happy to hear that Azrael completed his task! It's also a relief to know that Olympus has been destroyed. As Azrael likes to say,…"It was like a broken down motel on the edge of Vegas! "
As I imagine, I'm sure he felt he wouldn't make it.

There is also another issue I would like to address, which may make what you've all done seem like it was for nothing. During Io's pregnancy, she was coming to The Realm of the Forgotten, asking for large quantities of krythm. Since it doesn't effect her, I presume it was for her child. It may or may not kill the infant, but if the child survives, nonetheless, she'll be completely immune.

    I can't exactly prove who the father is, but my gut feeling is that it may be Zerachiel. He had a special attraction to her that he openly admitted to me, my friend.

    I've also talked to your Ya Ya. After explaining the current synopsis, with Io's mysterious pregnancy, she agrees that the father is more than likely Zerachiel.

    Don't worry about it now, you've got nearly two decades to show any concern. The child needs to be in between the ages of 16 and 18 to be an absolute threat to anyone. And as wishy washy as Io is, they may or may not discover what their body is capable of- And I do believe it's a girl. Maybe she'll listen a little better? Who knows.

I can't wait to meet up with the lot of you again. And I can't tell you how thankful I am that everything worked out in the end. Suppose what I've told you a small flaw working its way through the defects of life, and leave it at that! I highly doubt that Io is hardhearted enough to be vengeful, but it's best you keep your eyes open. Never settle when everything seems fine, if it's too quiet, someone is up to something!

Please tell everyone I miss them, and we'll have to meet up soon, my friend.

                        As always pleasure
                                Elmer

Made in the USA
Charleston, SC
17 October 2012